W9-AVR-671

She was afraid of the growing feelings she had for Andrei. Did he feel it too?

"Feel what?"

Her face heated, and she clamped a hand over her mouth. Obviously she'd spoken her fears aloud.

She let down her hand and said, "This thing between us."

"Yes, I feel it." The low rumble of his voice warmed the cool night air, filling the space between them with promise.

The baby kicked, inserting the silent reminder why Jocelyne couldn't have a relationship with any man. "Don't, Andrei."

Her voice came out as the barest of whispers she hoped he wouldn't hear. "Don't fall in love with me."

"I can't promise you that."

ELLE JAMES

UNDER SUSPICION, WITH CHILD

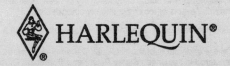

HARLEQUIN®

TORONTO • NEW YORK • LONDON
AMSTERDAM • PARIS • SYDNEY • HAMBURG
STOCKHOLM • ATHENS • TOKYO • MILAN • MADRID
PRAGUE • WARSAW • BUDAPEST • AUCKLAND

This book is dedicated to Harlequin Intrigue editors Allison Lyons and Sean Mackiewicz, whose vivid imaginations created the idea of Raven's Cliff, the curse and the intrigue. And thanks to the wonderful Harlequin authors who worked together to make this continuity come to life.

Special thanks and acknowledgment to Elle James for her contribution to The Curse of Raven's Cliff miniseries.

ISBN-13: 978-0-373-69347-4
ISBN-10: 0-373-69347-8

UNDER SUSPICION, WITH CHILD

www.eHarlequin.com

ABOUT THE AUTHOR

2004 Golden Heart Winner for Best Paranormal Romance, Elle James started writing when her sister issued the Y2K challenge to write a romance novel. She managed a full-time job, raised three wonderful children and she and her husband even tried their hands at ranching exotic birds (ostriches, emus and rheas) in the Texas hill country. Ask her and she'll tell you what it's like to go toe-to-toe with an angry 350-pound bird! After leaving her successful career in Information Technology Management, Elle is now pursuing her writing full-time. She loves building exciting stories about heroes, heroines, romance and passion. Elle loves to hear from fans. You can contact her at ellejames@earthlink.net or visit her Web site at www.ellejames.com.

Books by Elle James

HARLEQUIN INTRIGUE
 906—BENEATH THE TEXAS MOON
 938—DAKOTA MELTDOWN
 961—LAKOTA BABY
 987—COWBOY SANCTUARY
1014—BLOWN AWAY
1033—ALASKAN FANTASY
1052—TEXAS-SIZED SECRETS
1080—UNDER SUSPICION, WITH CHILD

CAST OF CHARACTERS

Andrei Lagios—Police Officer on the Raven's Cliff force whose younger sister was a victim of the Seaside Strangler.

Jocelyne Baker—Holistic healer and pregnant daughter of the town kook, enlisted as a cover story by Raven's Cliff police officer Lagios to assist in the search for the Seaside Strangler.

Hazel Baker—Warm-hearted, peace-loving town kook and owner of the Cliffside Inn, working through her Wicca beliefs to create a cure for the curse plaguing Raven's Cliff.

Mayor Perry Wells—Corrupt mayor of Raven's Cliff and a regular at the Cliffside Inn, suspected of taking kickbacks from an illegal source, also a bereaved father whose daughter disappeared on the day of her wedding.

Grant Bridges—Resident of the Cliffside Inn whose fiancée, the mayor's daughter, disappeared on the day of their wedding.

Rick Simpson—Mayor Wells's assistant and a regular at the Cliffside Inn, he's also a man with a hidden agenda.

Alex Gibson—Mild-mannered fisherman and resident of the Cliffside Inn who believes in Hazel Baker's search for the cure to the curse of Raven's Cliff.

Ingram Jackson—Solitary, wealthy recluse with severe burn scars who keeps to himself but frequents the Cliffside Inn for Hazel Baker's remedies.

Chapter One

The cool ocean breeze of summer feathered through the loose tendrils of Jocelyne Baker's hair, caressing her skin and body, soothing the tension away. Sitting with her legs crossed on the mat, her hands flat on the ground beside her, eyes closed, she inhaled, and let it out slowly.

All the tension of being cooped up for the past two rainy days in the inn with her mother melted away.

Maybe coming home hadn't been such a good idea. She could have made it work had she stayed in New Jersey. Somehow.

The flutter of tiny feet in her belly reminded her why she'd returned. Pregnant and alone, she'd needed a better place than the city to raise her child, even if it meant going home.

Breathe in, breathe out.

Nothing had changed. The town was as it had been when she'd left. Her mother was still considered the town kook and everyone stared at her, waiting for her to be just as flaky. *Like mother, like daughter.*

The only difference was that this time she was more mature, more confident in her own place in life. She refused to let whispering gossips hurt her or her child. Her muscles clenched in her neck and shoulders.

Breathe in, breathe out.

Moving back to Raven's Cliff wasn't a mistake. She repeated this mantra with each breath in and each one out.

Despite the cleansing breeze, other thoughts edged into her meditation. What of the Seaside Strangler? The man hadn't been caught. Would they catch him before Jocelyne brought her child into this world?

Unable to establish the inner peace she so intensely needed, Jocelyne pushed to her feet and stood straight, staring over the edge of the cliff out to the churning sea. Then she squatted, lowering her buttocks while her hands reached toward the sky, and closed together as if in prayer. Her hamstrings and the muscles in her back stretched, the tops of her thighs tingling with the effort to maintain the pose and tap in on the elusive inner peace she desperately sought.

HIS FEET POUNDING AGAINST the gravel, Andrei Lagios shut out everything but his breathing and the burning sensation in his muscles as he pushed himself harder and faster. He wanted the pain, even welcomed it. Pain reminded him he was alive. Unfortunately, so was the fiend who'd killed his beautiful little sister.

Despite the cool temperatures and the bite of the wind off the ocean, sweat leaked from every pore. Still he ran on, his lungs near bursting, but his attempts to turn off his memories failed. His thoughts mirrored the frothy, wind-tossed seas and the skies laden with heavy storm clouds.

He'd chosen the path along the cliff because no one would bother him here, and he felt closer to Sofia, who'd washed ashore near here two months ago. Her pale, bloated face and the seashell necklace around her throat still churned in Andrei's mind. He'd been the one on duty when the report came across the radio that the two girls who'd been missing since the night of their high-school prom had been found, washed against the rocky shoreline.

He'd been the one to break it to his parents that their only little girl, his younger sister, had died at the hands of the Seaside Strangler. The bitter truth burned in his chest that he had done nothing to stop the killer or keep him from doing it again.

Andrei couldn't run hard or fast enough to escape his failure. Someone in this small community had committed the crime and he hadn't found him yet.

In the distance, he spotted movement near the edge of the cliff overlooking the area where a tourist had discovered the girls' bodies.

Squinting against the wind, he tried to make out what it was. Then it moved again, rising from the ground, straightening. A woman wearing a white flowing skirt sat cross-legged, lifting her face to the sky. The wind whipped bright red strands of hair in Medusa-like fashion around her head.

His heart skipped several beats before shooting the blood through his body too fast for his veins to handle. Adrenaline sped his feet, kicking up chunks of gravel in his wake.

What was a woman doing out on the cliff alone? Hadn't she heard of the Seaside Strangler? And what was with the white dress?

If Andrei never saw another white dress, he'd be happy. To him, white meant death.

She rose to her feet, her posture straight as a pole, the sometimes gale-force winds twisting the ghostly pale skirt around her body, plastering it against her. Her blouse flapped, exposing the creamy fair skin of her hips and back. As though caught in a trance, she stared out toward the waves. Then she bent at the knees, her arms rising above her in the position of someone about to dive over the edge of a cliff.

Andrei's breath lodged in his throat for a brief second, then all the air in his lungs burst out on one word. "No!"

With the length of a football field between them, he knew

he couldn't stop her if she chose to dive onto the rocks below, but he had to try. Another woman couldn't die on his watch. He owed that much to Sofia and the people of Raven's Cliff.

The wind caught his words and whipped them away. Lifting his elbows and knees, he pumped harder, working his muscles to a screaming point. He'd never run so fast, nor felt so frustrated that he couldn't run faster.

The woman bent lower, tucking her head between her arms.

"Stop! Don't do it!" Andrei yelled again.

This time, she heard him and turned in his direction, her eyes wide, her mouth opened in an *O*. Her feet shifted and she stumbled on the gravel, tilting toward the edge of the cliff. The one-hundred-foot drop to the rocky shore below would be the death of her.

Desperation spurred Andrei on. "Don't jump! Please."

She righted herself, her brows knitting over her eyes. "Jump?"

Andrei ground to a stop in front of her, grasping her arms in a viselike grip. "Don't." He gasped, dragging air into his lungs before he could go on.

"Don't jump?" She stared at him, her smoky-green eyes troubled.

All Andrei could do was glance at the edge of the cliff as he hauled more air into his starving lungs.

Her brows lifted and the hint of a smile tilted the corners of her lips. "Oh, I get it. You think I was about to jump." She brought her hands up between his wrists, attempting to knock his fingers loose from her arms. When he didn't let go, her frown reappeared. "I assure you, I have no intention of jumping from this cliff or any other. You can let go of me, now."

He stared at her long and hard before he reluctantly released her. "Then why the hell did you look like you were about to dive?"

"Ah, the Utkatasana." She laughed, the sound like the tinkling bells of a wind chime.

"Utka-what?"

Her laughter disappeared, whipped away by the wind, but her sparkling green eyes continued to reflect her amusement. "Relax, cowboy. I wasn't about to dive, I was relaxing with one of my yoga positions. Utkatasana." Her knees bent and she raised her arms, her hands pressed together as if in prayer. "It's called the chair position. It's good for the arms, legs, diaphragm and heart."

Anger washed away any last trace of fear he might have felt and exploded in words. "Are you crazy?"

She winced, her full, luscious lips tightening into a thin line. "Excuse me?"

"For all I knew, you were about to throw yourself over the edge. And if you weren't out to kill yourself, you are definitely an easy target for the Seaside Strangler." He stepped closer, standing toe-to-toe with the fiery-haired woman. "Lady, go home. Go home and lock your doors." As soon as the words left his mouth, he knew he'd made a mistake.

Her eyes narrowed and she glared at him. "First of all, I don't take orders from you or anyone else. Second, I'm not crazy and I'll go wherever I want. Who do you think you are, telling me or anyone else what they can or can't do?"

"I'm a cop with the Raven's Cliff Police Department." Even to his own ears, his response was a lame excuse to be bossing the woman around.

"So?" She crossed her arms over her chest, a coppery brow rising high on her pale forehead. The stiff breeze lifted the ends of the filmy white skirt she wore, plastering it to her long, slender legs.

The dress reminded him of the dress his sister wore when she'd been found. A white wedding dress, not unlike what this woman wore. All the starch and anger drained from him. "Look, it's not safe for a lone woman to be out here."

"I can take care of myself." Her hand smoothed the dress

down over her belly. "I'm not suicidal, and I know what to look out for. I just wanted a little peace and quiet away from the inn."

So she was a tourist. A twinge of disappointment nudged at him. She wouldn't stay long at Raven's Cliff. But with a killer loose, leaving seemed the best idea.

Her determined stance and ability to stand up for herself had intrigued him more than he cared to admit. The way the filmy dress wrapped around her trim calves probably had something to do with the attraction as well.

He straightened, hardening his jaw. "Take a friend with you next time. We don't know who the strangler is and I'd hate to see you washed up on the rocks." *Like my sister*. He didn't say it, but he felt it with the pain in his chest.

"I've walked this path since I was a tiny girl. I know where all the hiding places are and believe me, there aren't many out here. And if I wanted to jump over the edge, I'd have done it already, and you couldn't have stopped me." She eased toward the edge.

His hand shot out automatically, grasping her arm.

"All right, already. I'm not going to jump. I was just going to show you that there is a path down the side of the cliff. If I wanted to go down, I'd walk."

Together they leaned over the edge and stared at the thin path that surely only a goat could traverse.

"I used to take it down to the water to find shells and starfish among the—" Her face paled to gray and she stumbled back against him. "Holy mother."

Andrei clasped her shoulders and set her behind him before peering over the edge to the rocks below.

Lifted by the waves and pushed into the rocks was the body of a woman dressed in white, facedown in the surf.

Chapter Two

Of all the stupid times to pass out, Jocelyne couldn't have picked a worse. But to wake up in the arms of this stranger... Shivers rippled over her entire body. And darn it all, they weren't shivers of fear.

A woman was dead at the bottom of the cliffs, for heaven's sake. Why should she be so concerned about being crushed against a man's brawny chest and carried away? They were headed toward town. How dangerous could that be?

She could smell the man's sweat and it was having an entirely unwarranted effect on her, driving her blood to pump faster, her heart to race and her skin to flush.

"Put me down." Jocelyne kicked her feet and pushed with her free hand against the man's well-muscled chest. The other hand wrapped around his neck to keep him from dropping her on the rocks. "We have to notify the police about that girl."

"That's where I'm headed." His feet ate the distance between the cliff and town in long easy strides.

"Look, for all I know you could be the Seaside Strangler." Her breath caught in her throat as his hand shifted, brushing against the underside of her breast. "Why else would you be out there?"

"I was jogging."

Okay, calm down. No need in upsetting the baby. On the

other hand, what did she really know about the muscle-bound man with the soulful dark eyes? So he was wearing a T-shirt, shorts and running shoes. The strangler could dress the same.

She renewed her struggles. "Put me down before I scream." With the wind blowing and still on the outskirts of town, she doubted anyone would hear her. But she'd give it her best effort. She dragged in a breath.

"If I were the Seaside Strangler, would I be carrying you toward town? To the Raven's Cliff Police Department?"

Her breath released in a huff. "If you wanted to throw people off your trail, maybe." As they entered town, the few cars driving along the road slowed.

Jocelyne groaned. "Put me down. People are pointing at us." She cupped his cheek and made him look at her. "Please?"

Something in her voice must have gotten to the Neanderthal and made him pause. "Are you sure you won't pass out again?"

She raised a hand scout-style. "I promise."

If his frown was any indication, he didn't quite believe her, but he let her feet drop to the ground, while retaining the arm around her waist.

"Look, I'm pregnant, not sick. The reason I passed out was that I haven't eaten breakfast." She patted his chest. "See? Easy fix. Now let me go."

A gaggle of women exiting the coffee shop a block away stopped and stared at Jocelyne and the man in the running shorts.

"I can manage it from here, *Officer*." Jocelyne's cheeks burned like they had when her classmates pointed and whispered about her mother being a witch, when they made taunts that she was the spawn of the devil. She turned toward the police department, but try as she might, she couldn't shake the cop's hand from her waist. "Really, I can walk on my own."

"Until we get you to the station, you'll have to deal with a little help."

One of the women leaned toward the ear of another, her gaze following Jocelyne's progression down the street, her lips moving fast.

"I don't like it when people stare," she whispered through her teeth.

"I don't care what they think. There's a dead woman back there, you passed out, and I'm not letting go of you until we get to the police station." His jaw could have been carved in granite, ebony eyes staring straight ahead unwavering from his course. That arm was like a steel band, locking her against his rock-solid side.

Jocelyne's heart hammered against her ribs. This man was hard, strong and determined. If he were the Seaside Strangler, she didn't stand a chance. Nor did any other woman. The fact he was a cop, didn't mean anything. There were such animals as renegade cops gone bad. Her instincts told her he wasn't bad and he wasn't the Seaside Strangler, but he also wasn't letting go of her. The fact that he'd carried her for almost half a mile impressed her. Not that she'd admit it to him.

A pretty young blonde stepped out of the beauty shop and waved at the man whose hand gripped dangerously close to Jocelyne's breast. "Hi, Andrei." Her face crinkled into a pout, her gaze narrowing at the hand around Jocelyne's waist. "Are we still on for tonight?"

"Sorry. Something's come up. I have to work." He passed her with little more than a glance, hurrying on to the stately brick building that housed not only the police station, but the jail and courthouse.

All along Main Street, Jocelyne reminded herself that the victim of the Seaside Strangler took precedence over her own embarrassed sensibilities. She could suffer through the inconvenience. Humiliation was a better alternative to what happened to that girl in the waves.

Once inside the building, Andrei settled her into a chair, with surprising gentleness. "Are you going to be okay?"

She inhaled the musky scent of male sweat, mingled with a hint of aftershave, and gulped. When he was being nice, he was almost handsome and sexy in his damp clothes, his thighs bulging from beneath his running shorts. "I'm fine," she lied. "It was just the shock." Seeing a body on the rocks, on top of being hungry and pregnant had caused her to black out. Having him stand so close, leaning all his bronzed muscles into her vision, just made her dizzier.

He stared hard at her, his brows drawing together. Had he read her mind? Could he see her reluctant attraction to him? Did he think less of her because she was pregnant and unmarried? She leaned back in her chair, determined to distance herself from him. Why should she care what he thought?

Her hand moved to the swell beneath her shirt. Because she kept in shape and had gained so little weight, she didn't look very pregnant...yet. As the next few weeks passed, her condition would only become more apparent.

"What's going on?" A bald man perhaps in his midfifties stepped through an open doorway, a coffee mug in one hand.

The man named Andrei straightened, his face drawn and tight. "Captain, I think we found Angela Wheeler."

The captain's gaze locked with Andrei's for a moment, then he sighed. "Where?"

"Washed up on the rocks below the cliffs north of town."

"Sure it wasn't the mayor's daughter?"

Andrei shook his head. "From where I stood, she looked tall, maybe five foot nine or ten. Camille was only five-four, right?"

"That's right." The captain nodded. "When did you find her?"

"Just a few minutes ago. I didn't have a chance to get a positive ID, but she had the long blond hair and looked to be tall and thin like the girl in the picture Angela's parents circulated."

"Damn." The older man turned toward the desk. "Joe, get the county coroner on the phone and send a squad car out to the cliffs north of town, we have another homicide." When he faced Andrei again, he asked, "Same MO?"

Andrei nodded. "White dress, washed up on shore."

"We'll get the state crime lab right out there." He shook his head. "This has got to stop. People can't feel safe in their homes or let their daughters out without being afraid of that maniac."

Andrei's hands tightened into fists. "We have to find him."

The captain laid a hand on Andrei's arm. "Sorry. I know what this means to you and I know how hard you've worked this case."

As the outsider looking in, Jocelyne didn't know what a stranger's death meant to the man who'd held her captive all the way back to town. By the whiteness of his fisted hands, she'd have to guess that it meant a lot.

Holding the coffee mug in one hand, the captain clutched the other hand to his gut. "This case is giving me an ulcer." He dug in his pocket and unearthed a roll of antacids, popping one into his mouth. He chewed and then washed it down with the last of the coffee.

Jocelyne cringed. "You know, if you cut back on the coffee and high-fat foods and go on a regimen of mastic gum, that ulcer might go away."

The man turned to Jocelyne, as if seeing her for the first time. "You think so? I'd give up my right arm to make my stomach feel better." He stared down into his mug, then up at her. "Who are you?"

She stuck out her hand. "Jocelyne Baker. I'm a holistic healer. You know...natural cures versus surgery and drug company medications."

"Captain Patrick Swanson." The older man's brows rose. "Mastic gum? Where do I find that?"

"At any health food store or you can get it from me. I keep

a stock of natural products and herbs. It's my business." She waited for the usual frown to appear on the man's face, but was surprised when he smiled.

"If you could fix me up with something to cure this pain in my gut, I'd be forever grateful." He rubbed his belly and groaned. "This case isn't helping."

"I'll have some mastic gum capsules to you before the end of the day. Just as soon as I dig some out of my packing boxes."

"Great." Captain Swanson glanced at Andrei, his face drawn and showing his age. "For now, we have a murder to solve, don't we?"

Jocelyne took the opportunity to escape while Andrei wasn't physically stopping her. "If you don't need me anymore, I'll be on my way."

The captain redirected his attention to her. "I'll have questions for you later, after we recover the body. You don't have plans to leave town, do you?"

"No, I'm here for an extended stay. You can reach me at the Cliffside Inn. Tell you what, come by later with your questions, and I'll have your mastic gum."

"Are you a guest there?" he asked.

A twinge of disappointment squeezed Jocelyne's chest. The older man hadn't remembered her. What did she expect? As a teenager, she'd done her best to be invisible, wearing drab clothing and a hat over her brilliant red hair. Not until she'd moved away from Raven's Cliff had she had the courage to be herself. "No. I live there."

"Do I know you?" The captain's eyes narrowed. "Baker, huh? Any relation to Hazel?"

Jocelyne inhaled and let it out. She was an adult now, and she could handle any ridicule thrown her way. "She's my mother."

"Ah, the innkeeper's daughter." He nodded, a smile softening his face. "I thought you looked familiar. I'd heard you'd come back to Raven's Cliff. Well then, good. I'll know where to look when I need to ask questions."

She nodded, a swell of relief rushing over her. "Then I'll be on my way."

A large, calloused hand clamped onto her arm. "I'm taking you there." Andrei's chin set in a hard line.

The hairs on the back of her neck bristled. For the past ten years, she'd been independent of anyone telling her what to do. Even the two men in her life hadn't interfered with her decisions. But with a body lying at the base of Raven's Cliff, she didn't want to make it a big deal.

With firm resolve, she peeled his hand off her arm. "No. You have much more important things to do. I'll be fine on my own." That said, she left, refusing to give him the opportunity to argue.

Having lost her sandals somewhere along the cliff, Jocelyne walked barefoot, her feet more tender than when she was a girl. The day was dreary, with clouds hanging low on the horizon and no sun to cast shadows or shed light into dark corners.

She hurried past the shops, hoping she didn't bump into anyone else before she got home. All her old insecurities about being the village kook's daughter surfaced to haunt her every step.

The Cliffside Inn stood near the town square, stately and welcoming after the horror of finding a woman's dead body floating in the surf. Until she reached the inn, she'd felt fine. Numb, but fine. As soon as her feet touched the first step, her knees shook. By the time she opened the door, her entire body shook.

When all she wanted to do was go up to her room and collapse across her bed, she knew she couldn't. Her baby needed nourishment. She had to get food in her stomach, even if eating was the last thing she wanted to do. This living being growing inside relied on her to care for him or her. This baby had not yet been introduced to this cold, callous world, where a woman wasn't safe even in a small peaceful town like Raven's Cliff.

Tears stung Jocelyne's eyes. What a world to bring a child into. Had her curse followed her back to Raven's Cliff?

When her first lover died seven years ago, she'd attributed it to bad luck that he'd been run over by a city bus. When the father of her unborn child fell on the subway tracks and was crushed by several tons of train, Jocelyne had thought long and hard. The common denominator was that they both loved her. Nothing else about their lives was the same. They had different occupations, different looks and different philosophies. But they'd dared to love her.

Despite her desire to put her mother's Wicca beliefs behind her, Jocelyne couldn't help but wonder if there was truth in the saying, Nothing is ever a coincidence. All actions, all events have a purpose.

With the death of Tyler Reed, her baby's father, and newly pregnant, Jocelyne had struggled to hold it together. In the end, she was drawn back to where her troubles began. Maybe if she resolved her anger with her mother, the rest of her life would get better and the curse would lift. She hoped so for the sake of her unborn child.

The image of a girl dressed in white, lying at the bottom of the cliff, stabbed at her empty stomach, making it knot in pain. So far it looked as though her curse had followed her and extended beyond men who loved her. Was she destined to be followed by a black cloud of doom?

AFTER SPENDING THE DAY watching the state crime team comb the cliffs and the rocky shore below, Andrei was physically and emotionally exhausted. But he couldn't stop until he found the murderer. He owed it to Sofia, his beautiful little sister who'd been the third victim of the Seaside Strangler.

Angela's body had been recovered before noon and taken

directly to the coroner where an autopsy was begun immediately. Mayor Wells had been there holding his breath when they pulled her from the surf, his face gray and lined with worry. Only when they turned her over and proved for certain she was Angela, did he draw in a shaky breath and run a hand through his thick, graying hair, standing it on end. He'd left shortly afterward, without a word to the captain, disappearing from the scene like a ghost.

Andrei knew what the medical examiner would say. Died of strangulation by a necklace of rare seashells. The same fate as his sister, her friend Cora and Rebecca Johnson.

Failure ate at his gut, stirring his anger. No clues had surfaced thus far to point the police force in the right direction. No fingerprints, no DNA samples from the attacker. Nothing. In a small community like Raven's Cliff, it shouldn't be so hard to find a killer.

But for the past several months, the perpetrator had eluded detection, slipped through their grasp and killed again.

Ten o'clock at night, and having sat at his desk for the past three hours, Andrei tapped a pencil to the file before him. The file he'd compiled and studied over the past couple months until he could recite every word, describe every picture. In it were the happy, unmarred faces of the women who'd died and the pictures taken after their bodies were discovered. A morbid before and after testimony to the killer's impact.

After interviewing family, friends and acquaintances, Andrei had determined that none of the victims had enemies sufficiently angry with them. At least not enough to warrant killing them.

So far, the killer preyed on young women, yet none of the women had shown signs of rape. All of them had been dressed in white wedding gowns, strangled and thrown into the sea. What was the connection to the young women, the white wedding dresses and the sea? The whole situation reeked of sacrifices. Some sick ritual dreamed up by a demented mind.

A chill slithered down the back of Andrei's neck.

Who would he target next?

His thoughts drifted to the woman he'd found by the cliffs. The image of Jocelyne Baker, pregnant, standing straight, facing the ocean, the wind whipping her dress against her thighs swam through his mind. God, he hated to think of finding her facedown in the water, her fiery-red hair floating around her pale face. Andrei clenched his fist, the pencil between his fingers snapping in two.

So far, the maniac had preyed on unmarried, young women, but that didn't mean he wouldn't take a pregnant one. He needed to stop by the inn and stress the importance of personal safety to Ms. Baker. Not that she'd listen to him. But maybe for the sake of her unborn child she'd hear what he had to say. He glanced at his watch.

"Go home." Captain Swanson stepped up to Andrei's desk. "Get some rest. You look all done in."

"I have to figure this out." He slammed the broken pencil into the trash bin beside his desk.

"You've been on it for months. Hell, the entire force has been on it for months and we've found nothing."

Andrei pounded the middle of the file with his fist. "Another girl died on our watch, damn it."

"Take it easy, Lagios." The captain laid a hand on Andrei's shoulder. "You didn't kill her. It's not your fault."

"It's my fault I didn't catch him before he struck again. It's my fault I didn't catch him before he took my sister and her friend."

"We don't have anything to go on. This guy isn't leaving us a bone to gnaw on."

"Then we have to interview every last person in this town, knock on every door, search every closet, basement and attic until we find something."

"We can't do that. People have rights."

Andrei pushed to his feet so fast, his chair fell over backward. "What about Sofia's rights? Or Angela's or Cora's? They had the right to live and he took that right away from them."

"You know the law. We can't search houses without probable cause and a search warrant."

"To hell with search warrants. We have a killer to catch before he does it again." Andrei's lips pressed together and he breathed fast, exhaling through his nose. He wouldn't let the bastard kill again—he couldn't. "We have to be missing something. Some small trace of evidence that will lead us to the suspect."

"This is his fourth victim, he has to slip up sometime."

As the last statement left the captain's mouth, the phone on Andrei's desk rang. Could he dare to hope it was a sign?

Andrei lifted the phone. "Lagios."

"Andrei, this is Gordon Fennell, I think I might have found something."

"Are you done with the autopsy, already?" Andrei glanced up at Swanson. "Wait. I have the captain here. Let me put you on speakerphone." He punched the button and laid the receiver on its rest. "Go ahead."

"First of all, the victim has the same markings as the others. The same seashell necklace strung together on generic fishing line. She's wearing a wedding dress that could have been bought in a resale shop anywhere in Maine."

Tension built behind Andrei's temples as the medical examiner listed what Andrei already knew. He resisted the urge to tell the man to cut to the chase.

"Everything points to the same attacker."

"What is it you found?" the captain asked.

Andrei held his breath, hoping this would be the big break they were looking for.

"A trace of a chemical found in her bloodstream. I retested blood from the other three victims and found it in their blood as well."

"What is it?"

"From what I could tell, it's a chemical that comes from the henbane plant, not something you find around these parts on a regular basis. In some places it's illegal to grow."

Andrei leaned toward the speakerphone. "What does it do?"

"In smaller doses, it's considered a painkiller or hallucinogen. In larger doses, it'll kill. Although there wasn't enough concentration in their blood to kill them, it would certainly have made them very high, docile and malleable."

Andrei sat back, his mind wrapping around this new information. "Where would someone get this drug?"

The medical examiner paused before answering. "They don't sell it in the drugstore, that's for sure. And you can't just order it online. Someone would have to grow the plant itself. Someone with an herb garden, possibly in a greenhouse."

Silence stretched over a full minute before Gordon broke the tension. "That's all the new information I have. I still have a few more things to check. Hope it helps."

"Thanks, Gordon. It helps." The captain hit the off button and stared down at the phone for several long moments. "Who has a greenhouse or herb garden in this area?"

Andrei's mind wrapped around the knowledge that an herb was used in drugging the young women. The only person he knew who might understand the use of herbs was the woman he'd met this morning beside the cliff. "How long has Jocelyne Baker been back in town?"

Captain Swanson shook his head. "Not long enough to have committed the first three murders. Besides, she's in good shape, but she's not strong enough to strangle a full grown young woman, drugged or not."

"Yeah, besides, she's pregnant." He glanced up at the captain. "Where's the husband?"

"She told me that she came back alone. The father of her child isn't part of her picture. Whatever that means."

So she wasn't married. A swell of relief filled Andrei's conscience, and he quickly downplayed it. Not that he was interested in the strong-willed Jocelyne Baker. Although it was sad to think she'd be faced with raising her child alone.

Swanson tapped a finger to his chin. "Miss Baker might be a good source to consult over the use of this herb, henbane. Being a holistic healer, she'd have a good understanding of the chemical properties of natural substances."

Andrei stood and stretched the kinks out of his back. "I'll drop by the inn tomorrow and see if she knows anything. Maybe she can point to the nearest greenhouse or herb garden. After all, she'll be looking for a new source of the herbs she uses in her business."

Jocelyne Baker might be strong-willed, but Andrei couldn't see her as a murderer. With nothing else to go on, he needed a straw to grasp and she was his straw. He had to find the murderer for his sister. If getting close to Jocelyne helped him in his search, then he'd stick to her like duct tape.

"I was by there earlier to get her statement and that mastic gum, so be forewarned she might be leery of another cop snooping around." He patted his belly. "So far the stuff she gave me seems to be working. My stomach doesn't hurt nearly as bad."

Andrei's lips twitched. The woman knew her stuff and she knew her mind. She'd given as good as she got when he'd held her against her will by the cliff. She sure as hell wouldn't make it easy on him if he came around asking more questions. He'd have to come up with some way of making her want to help him. Make it sound like her idea. He'd have to turn on the Lagios killer charm.

The captain turned toward the door, stopped and glanced back. "While you're at it, check out her mother."

Andrei glanced up from plotting the strategy he'd use on

the lovely Jocelyne, suddenly anxious to get started. "Isn't she the one everyone thinks is a witch?"

"Yeah." The captain's eyes narrowed. "She might just be crazy enough to be in cahoots with the killer."

Chapter Three

A restless night's sleep did nothing to refresh Jocelyne's mind or body. Her dreams had been full of the overwhelming sense of fear. Dark clouds churned the sky and some unknown hand stirred the sea into a slate-gray froth of swells, the waves slapping against the rocky shoreline.

In the relative safety of her childhood home, a dark stranger lurked in the shadows of the Cliffside Inn, waiting to strangle her and toss her into the sea. She'd been wearing the white skirt she'd worn yesterday, almost like the one the dead girl in the water had been wearing. Two times in the middle of the night, she'd awoken drenched in sweat as if she'd been running. The baby kicked in protest, recognizing its mother's distress. Exhausted and dispirited from lack of sleep, Jocelyne gave up near dawn and climbed out of bed. She went to her computer, answering e-mails and responding to orders for her herbal remedies.

A couple hours later, the smell of bacon, eggs and homemade biscuits drifted through to her upstairs bedroom, reminding her of her need to nourish the growing child in her belly. Despite her intent to remain aloof from other boarders and guests of the inn, Jocelyne couldn't resist the breakfast call and descended to the bottom floor.

In the kitchen, with an apron tied around her gently

rounded figure, her long, fading red hair neatly twisted into a knot on top of her head, Hazel Baker scrambled eggs in a large skillet. "Oh, good, you're awake. Could you hand me that bowl on the counter over there?"

Jocelyne settled into the routine she'd grown up with, helping her mother cater to the guests that made living in the huge old mansion possible. "What can I do to help?"

"Mr. Gibson likes toast instead of biscuits. Would you pop two slices in the toaster?"

"Yes, ma'am."

Her mother scraped the eggs off the bottom of the pan and flipped them, careful not to brown the pale yellow. "You look tired, dear. Are you not feeling well?"

"I couldn't sleep." Jocelyne slid two slices of bread into the toaster and prayed her mother wouldn't question her too much on her dreams.

Hazel's hands paused in stirring the eggs. "I'm not sure now was a good time for you to come home, honey."

A lump settled in the empty cavity of Jocelyne's belly. "What do you mean?" After all these years, she'd come home to mend fences and wash away all the built-up resentment of her childhood. And now her mother was trying to get rid of her?

"What with the curse and all, it's just not safe for you and my grandbaby." Her mother stared across the hardwood floors of the kitchen at Jocelyne, her gaze dropping to her daughter's midsection before she turned back to the eggs. "Maybe you should go back to New Jersey."

Her words hit with the force of a baseball bat to Jocelyne's chest. "I can't, Mom. I don't have a home to go to. I gave up the lease on my apartment and I have my entire inventory here. I don't have any other home. Raven's Cliff is the only home I have left."

"Don't you have a friend you can stay with until after the

baby is born? Maybe by then I'll have come up with a cure for the curse."

Jocelyne pulled the slices from the toaster and carefully laid them on a plate. Then she dusted the crumbs from her fingers and walked across the kitchen to where her mother scraped the eggs into a large serving tray. When she set the pan in the sink, Jocelyne stood in front of her. "What curse are you talking about?"

"Captain Raven's curse, of course."

"The one about Beacon Lighthouse? I thought that was an old fish story."

Her mother's eyes widened. "Oh, no, my dear. Captain Raven left strict instructions that the lighthouse was to be lit and pointed to the exact position where his ship went down. He lost his entire family in that wreck, all those years ago."

"So where does the curse come in?"

"The Sterling family kept the promise to shine the light on that day until five years ago. Young Nicholas Sterling the Third…forgot." Her mother's voice softened, her eyes became sadder.

Despite her determination not to let her mother's superstitions affect her, Jocelyne couldn't stop the goose bumps rising across her arms.

"When his grandfather saw that the light wasn't lit, he climbed the steps himself, but it was too late. In his attempt to light the flame, he started a fire that destroyed the lighthouse. Nicholas tried to rescue his grandfather from the inferno, but he fell into the sea. It was all so horrible and his body was never recovered." Her mother buried her face in her hands, her shoulders shaking.

The older woman had bought into the curse with all her heart. Jocelyne pulled her mother into her arms and held her, rubbing her back until the sobs diminished. When Hazel raised her head, tears trembled on faded red lashes, her pale skin splotchy and wet, emphasizing the crow's feet at the corners of her eyes and the worry lines on her forehead. "I missed you, sweetie, but I'm so afraid for you."

"Don't worry about me, Mom. I can take care of myself. Why don't you go lie down and let me finish getting the breakfast out on the table?"

"Oh, no, you're the one who's pregnant. You should go put your feet up. I'll be all right." She wiped the tears from her face with the corner of her apron.

"I'm pregnant, not crippled. I'm in better physical shape than I've ever been." Jocelyne gently pried the spatula from her mother's hand. "Let me help. It's the least I can do to repay you for giving me a home to come to."

"You're always welcome, dear. This will always be your home. I just wish it was safe for you and your baby." Her mother wiped her hands down the front of her apron and stared around the kitchen. "The biscuits will need to come out of the oven in a few minutes. Don't forget the pancakes in the warmer."

"I can find things, go lie down." Jocelyne steered her mother toward the dining room.

Leah Toler was busy setting out napkin-wrapped silverware at each place setting. "Morning, Jocelyne."

"My mother is going to lie down for a few minutes. I'll be handling the kitchen duties." She gave her mother a stern stare. "We'll do just fine. Now go."

"I'm not used to letting someone else handle the kitchen."

"Then get used to having a little more help around here." Jocelyne smiled at Leah to let her know her comment wasn't meant to belittle Leah's work. She'd been a godsend to her mother.

Once her mother was out of the dining area, Jocelyne turned to push the swinging door into the kitchen. At the same time, the door swung toward her, jamming her hand. Pain shot through her wrist and she jumped back. "Ouch!"

Rick Simpson strode into the dining room from the kitchen. "I'm sorry, did I hurt you?" He grabbed her hand and held it, studying her wrist for a brief second. His hands were cool and clammy like beached fish.

Jocelyne jerked her fingers out of his grasp. "I'm fine, you just surprised me. Most guests enter through the front door." If her voice was sharp, count it up to the shards of pain shooting through her jammed fingers.

"So they do." Simpson's attention moved from her to the breakfast buffet set up against the wall of the large dining room. Without another word, he stepped around Jocelyne and lifted a plate so that he could be first in line when the food came out.

Jocelyne used her other hand to push the swinging door. "Jerk," she muttered beneath her breath as she strode across the kitchen, shaking the kink out of her damaged hand.

"I hope you're not referring to me."

The voice behind her made her jump. "Don't do that!" She faced the man who'd occupied much of her thoughts yesterday and most of last night in her dreams. If not for him, her nightmares would have been much worse, but that didn't excuse him sneaking up on her.

He leaned against a counter, incredibly handsome in his police uniform.

"Guests enter through the front door, not the kitchen." She marched to the oven and pulled out the tray of biscuits, ignoring the tingle of awareness she'd felt at his nearness.

"I'm not here to eat." Andrei Lagios pushed away from the counter he leaned against and moved toward her, gliding like a jaguar toward his prey.

Had heat from the open oven caused the temperature to rise so dramatically in the room? Jocelyne stood in his path, her gaze fixed on his mesmerizing dark eyes. Not until heat seeped through the hot pad did she return to her senses. "Yow!" She looked for a place to set the hot tray but the countertops were full of the dishes to be carried to the dining room.

Andrei snatched an oven mitt from a hook on the wall and relieved Jocelyne of the laden cookie sheet. "Do you have a basket you want to put these in?"

"Uh, yes. Of course." She scrambled for her wits and the basket her mother had set out. After laying a colorful cloth on the bottom and draping it over the side, she plucked each fluffy biscuit from the pan and dropped it into the basket, all the while gathering her thoughts. "Did you have further questions for me, or is this a social visit?"

"Questions."

A small part of her that she had thought buried poked its disappointed head up. She squashed it down and dropped the last biscuit into the basket. "You can put the pan in the sink."

While Andrei's back was turned, Jocelyne took the opportunity to study the man who'd carried her most of the way back to town yesterday. Encased in a sexy blue-gray uniform shirt, his impossibly broad shoulders all but filled the air in the spacious kitchen. No wonder he could carry not only a woman, but a pregnant woman that far and not look the least worn out. He was a cop, he probably worked out on a regular basis. Jet-black hair was longer than what she'd consider regulation for a man in his profession, but then it made him look more dangerous, a rule breaker. And the eyes—

He chose that moment to face her and pin her with his ebony gaze. "I found out something interesting yesterday you might be able to help me with."

"Me? I've been out of this town for close to ten years. I barely know anyone. How could I possibly help?" And she didn't want to spend any more time than she had to with this man who made her feel strangely off balance.

Leah poked her head through the swinging door. "Better hurry with the food. The natives are restless."

"You're busy, let me help you get this food out before your customers start shouting." He lifted a tray of scrambled eggs and the basket of biscuits and left the room through the swinging doors.

More intrigued than she cared to admit, Jocelyne grabbed the pancakes out of the warmer and the tray of condiments and followed. What had he found and why come to her?

ANDREI STOOD BACK WHILE Jocelyne arranged the food on the buffet, placing serving spoons and spatulas within easy reach. He admired her smooth efficiency and easy smile for the guests, finding himself envious of her attention.

The customers waited patiently in line until she'd finished. Andrei, with less patience than the hungry patrons, stood by the kitchen door, arms crossed over his chest, his toe tapping the wood flooring of the elegant old house. He'd been here for breakfast on one or two occasions, but he wasn't here about food. He was here on business. Although the scent of bacon and pancakes were making his mouth water.

Finally, Jocelyne stood back and announced, "Help yourselves." With that she grabbed her hot pads and hurried toward the kitchen, leaving the pretty blond worker to fill glasses.

Andrei held the door for her and as soon as it closed behind them, he dug in his pocket and pulled out a piece of paper. "Are you familiar with a plant called henbane?"

Jocelyne reached for the color picture of an ordinary-looking plant. "A little. I know that it's dangerous. A person can die if given a lethal quantity. The pagans used it in Medieval Europe as a painkiller and sometimes as a poison...." She glanced up at him. "Why do you ask?"

"Do you know of anyone who might have access to it?"

Her brows drew together and her teeth chewed on her bottom lip. "It's not something you can find easily in the

States—" Jocelyne froze, her eyes widened and she shook her head. "No way. She wouldn't."

"Who wouldn't what?"

She spun on her heels and flew toward a door at the opposite end of the kitchen, flinging it wide to reveal the entrance to a lower level beneath the house. Before he could stop her, she was racing down the steps into the darkness.

For a split second, panic seized Andrei's chest and he rushed for the doorway, staring down into pitch black. A light flickered below and Jocelyne's silhouette appeared.

"Wait." He took the steps two at a time, catching the bottom step with the edge of his heel, stumbling before he could right himself.

The innkeeper's red-haired daughter was nowhere in sight, but her footsteps echoed against the damp walls.

In the back corner of the sprawling subterranean room were long tables stretched out beneath fluorescent lights. Jocelyne hurried along the rows of greenery flourishing in the underground greenhouse.

Was she on to something? Had she found his source of the drug used on the four victims of the Seaside Strangler? Andrei hurried to catch up to her.

When she stopped before one plant, her face turned an alarming shade of white. "This is it…" Her voice came out in a whisper and she handed him the sheet of paper, pointing to the plant that was the exact replica of the picture he'd pulled from the Internet. "This is henbane."

"Well, Ms. Baker. Seems we have a problem."

"Oh, Mom, why do you have such a dangerous plant?" The self-assured and self-proclaimed independent woman, who'd had Andrei scratching his head since he'd met her, turned a sickly pale green and sank toward the floor in a dead faint.

Chapter Four

Strong, warm arms held her against a solid wall of muscles. Seems she'd been here before. Jocelyne opened her eyes and stared up into dark brown eyes, hooded in the shadows of the overhead lights. "Did I do it again?"

"Uh-huh." He pushed a strand of her hair away from her face. "You're not such a good advertisement for a holistic healer."

"Shut up." She pushed away from him and attempted to stand. Her knees refused to hold her weight and she fell back into Andrei's lap. Despite the coolness of the basement's musty interior, her cheeks heated. "My blood sugar must be low." Only a healthy breakfast and maybe some dry toast would make her better.

He set her to the side on the cool stone flooring and rose to his feet, extending a hand to her. "How many months along are you?"

In one swift tug, he had her up on her feet.

The rush of air in her face and blood to her legs made her stagger and fall against his chest. "What business is it of yours?"

"A man kinda likes to know a few details when the woman with him faints into his arms. Twice."

Jocelyne pushed away from him and smoothed a hand over the baby growing inside. "Six months. I'm six months along."

"And the father?"

"Dead."

"I'm sorry." And the bad thing was that he really did look sorry. The grow lights cast a reflection in his dark eyes, turning them to glowing ink.

"Me, too." She'd just discovered she was pregnant the day before he'd been killed in a subway accident. They'd only been engaged for one night. Before she found out she was pregnant, she'd been considering moving out because the spark wasn't there anymore for her. Had there ever really been a spark, or had she settled for companionship over coming home to an empty room?

"Jocelyne?" Andrei bent and peered into her face. "Are you sure you're all right?"

She pushed a stray hair out of her face, sweeping aside six-month-old memories with the wave of her hand. "Yes, yes. I'm all right."

His eyes narrowed as if he didn't believe her, but he straightened and stared back toward the corner lit by the grow lamps. "Unless you know of another local source of that plant, I'd venture to guess that someone has been harvesting from this garden to drug the victims."

Jocelyne stared at the lighted corner, uncontrollable cold overwhelming her body, almost as if a hideous creature lurked in the dark corners poised to crawl out after unsuspecting young women. She used to play hide-and-seek down here. Now all she could think of was the monster who could have been sneaking in to steal her mother's herbs. A shiver shook her so hard, her teeth rattled. "You don't think my mother's capable of murder, do you?"

Andrei shook his head. "The victims were all strangled. It takes a lot of strength to strangle someone and then load them into a boat."

"My mother is strong." She didn't know why she was

giving him reasons to suspect her mother. The townsfolk already thought Hazel was a nutcase. Had she crossed the line of mild mannered to murderer?

"But she probably doesn't have the strength it takes to lift a body. No, she's not the killer, although it doesn't take a lot of strength to be an accomplice."

"As much as my mother loves this town, I can't see her hurting anyone in it. If she is an accomplice to murder, she probably doesn't know it."

"Based on our brief acquaintance, I don't think your mother has it in her to hurt others."

He strode the full length of the basement level, studying the steps and the small windows positioned high on the walls that were on ground level from the outside. Very little light leached in through the dirty panes, casting a hazy glow two to three feet out from the glass. "Is there any other way in or out of here, besides the steps coming down from the kitchen?"

"No." Jocelyne followed Andrei, her head reeling with the possibilities. "As big as the basement is, it only has the one set of steps down into it."

"I don't think a grown man could crawl in and out of the windows, but I'll have a look at them from the outside."

"So, you think someone has been sneaking down here stealing my mother's herbs?" She leaned on a sturdy wood floor joist attempting a casual pose, when all she really needed was something to hold her up from the bombardment of frightening thoughts bearing down on her. "Who?"

"Good question. Does your mother lock the basement door?" Andrei stood with his back to the steps leading up to the kitchen.

"Only at night. It's left open during the day. We keep extra supplies and spices down here." She pointed to a shelf near the staircase stacked neatly with linens, pantry staples and bins of potatoes, carrots and onions. "Anyone could come down here."

Andrei scanned the contents briefly before his glance shifted back to the staircase. "We'll need to make a list of people who frequent the inn."

"Besides the tourists, there are quite a few Raven's Cliff residents who come here on a regular basis, not to mention the boarders who live here at the inn." She reached around him for a pad of paper kept on the shelf. Caught up in trying to remember every person who could have come down these steps, she didn't realize how close she'd come to the cop. As her hand closed around the pad, her breast bumped into the man's rock-solid chest, sending what could only be described as an electric jolt through her system.

Startled by her reaction, Jocelyne jumped back, the pad clattering to the floor. "I'm sorry. I'll just—" She bent to retrieve the pad, her cheeks burning, but Andrei's hand was there first and she touched the back of his long, sturdy fingers. Another shock raced through her hand up into her arm and she lurched backward into a stack of baskets, sending them toppling over onto the stone floor. When her foot hooked a basket handle she pitched forward, landing hard against the person she'd been struggling to get away from.

Andrei caught her, a low chuckle rumbling in his chest. "Are you always this nervous around men?"

"No." *Not men. Just you.* What was it about Andrei Lagios that had her flustered so badly she was either fighting mad, passing out or panting? Whatever it was, it had to stop. She wasn't interested in this or any man for that matter. Heck, she was six months pregnant and probably looked like she'd swallowed a basketball. What man would be attracted to that?

Jocelyne squared her shoulders and stepped free of Andrei's hands. "I'll make that list for you. Upstairs."

When she emerged from the darkened staircase into the well-lit kitchen, she inhaled the fresh, reassuring scent of biscuits, cleansing her senses of the cobwebs of the basement and the confusion of stumbling into the cop. For several long moments she stood breathing in and out until she had her body and mind calm and in control.

A strong hand on her arm sent all her control flying out the window. "You need to eat something before you pass out again."

"I will, just as soon as I jot down the names of the people I can remember."

"Tell you what." He led her to the table and urged her into a chair. "You sit. I'll get you a plate of food while you write that list. Then you can tell me all about it while you eat."

Before she could protest, the door swung closed behind the infuriating man.

Jocelyne could take care of herself. She didn't need a man waiting on her or treating her like she was fragile or unable to fend for herself. She was an expectant mother and soon would have a baby to look after. She'd darn well better get tough to take care of her child. Pulling her thoughts out of the dining room, where Andrei gathered food, she set a pen to the paper and wrote.

In a few minutes, she had half a page of names. All people she knew or had grown up with. The acids roiled in her empty belly, a sinking feeling killing her appetite. Was the Seaside Strangler one of them?

Her hand hovered over the names of people she knew who frequented the inn. By the time Andrei returned with a plate of scrambled eggs and toast and set it down beside her, she'd finished, the effort exhausting her more than she wanted to admit.

Andrei leaned over her shoulder and peered down at the list.

His proximity made her nerves jangle. The thought of a killer amongst them, coupled with a hunky cop hanging over her shoulder, gave her a panic attack that threatened to overwhelm her. She pushed back, bumping into Andrei as she rose. "I need to finish with the breakfast crowd."

Andrei handed her the plate. "Take the food with you. You need to eat." When she took the plate, his hand fell to her arm. "Let's keep this between the two of us. The less people who know about the henbane the better chance we have of finding our killer."

"What about my mother?"

"Promise me you won't tell anyone, including her."

She nodded, her stomach knotting into a tight clench. If she didn't get some food in her empty stomach, she'd embarrass herself in front of him.

"Eat. We'll talk later." He dropped his hand from her arm and left the kitchen through the back door.

ANDREI STRODE INTO THE RCPD half an hour later, a scowl marring his brow. "Captain!"

"In here!" Captain Swanson shouted from inside his office.

Without acknowledging the other policemen scattered around the building, Andrei made a beeline for the captain, entering his office without waiting to be invited. After he closed the door behind him, he paced in front of his supervisor's desk. "I found the source."

The captain leaned forward. "So soon?"

"Hazel Baker has an herb garden in the basement of Cliffside Inn." Andrei stopped pacing and faced him. "Henbane is one of the herbs she grows in that garden."

"Hazel Baker." Captain Swanson leaned back in his chair and scrubbed a hand down his face. "Half the town thinks she's crazy, but she can't be the killer. Our only surviving victim identified the Seaside Strangler as definitely male."

She had been the intended second victim of the Seaside Strangler but, fortunate for her, she escaped.

"That's right. However the basement isn't locked during the day. Anyone with knowledge of the hallucinogenic qualities of the henbane could have stolen leaves from that plant."

"Question is who?" The captain pinched the bridge of his nose.

Andrei pulled a folded piece of paper from his front breast pocket and tossed it on the desk. "That's a list of people who frequent the inn and the reasons they do, along with the current residents. We need to interview every one of them and get their whereabouts on the nights of Angela's, Cora's and my sister's disappearances. And we need to canvass the staff."

Just the thought of his sister, Sofia, caused a surge of anger and pain to well up in Andrei's throat. He swallowed hard past the knot of emotion, the backs of his eyelids burning. Even if he'd wanted to continue, he couldn't. Instead he grappled with the grief and impotent fury, his fists clenched with the need to kill the man who'd taken the life of his sweet little sister.

Swanson stared down at the list and whistled. "This is a pretty comprehensive list. We'll get started on the interviews right away. I'll have Mitch Chapman go after the two boarders, the fisherman Alex Gibson and Assistant DA Grant Bridges. Grant won't be happy, but too bad. I'll take Mayor Wells and his assistant, Rick Simpson, myself. They're touchy about everything since Perry admitted to taking illegal bribes. Not to mention his acquittal in Theodore Fisher's murder." Captain Swanson snorted. "Hard to believe a public servant in his position would be so low."

"Unfortunately, it happens all too often. But I know what you mean. It's disappointing when an elected official, responsible for upholding the laws, not only bends but breaks them."

"It gives people the impression that politicians think they're above the law." For a long moment the captain stared at the list. When he looked up at Andrei, a steely glint shone in his eyes. "This is the first real lead we've had in this case. This could be the break we need." He smacked his palm to the desk.

Andrei nodded.

"I want you to become a permanent fixture inside Cliff-side Inn. I don't care how you do it, but you need to find out who's been stealing the plant and nail him."

The potential for action cleared the blockage in Andrei's throat, his blood humming in anticipation of capturing the bastard who'd killed Sofia. "Any suggestions on how I'll hang out at the inn without alerting whoever it is to the fact I'm on to him? Send a cop in there and he'll back off."

The captain planted his elbows on the desk and steepled his fingers, his brows dipping low. For two long minutes he sat without speaking.

Ready to rush out and shake the truth out of people, Andrei had to put a cap on his aggression. Instead of marching down to the inn and blowing any chance of making this work, he turned and resumed pacing the length of the office. How could he get inside without tipping off the murderer? For that matter, how could he stay away? There were other women at risk at the inn should the killer strike again.

An image of the beautiful Jocelyne appeared in his head. He could still feel the warmth of her breast pressed against his chest. He was surprised a line hadn't formed outside the inn. A line of men ready to date the pretty redhead. Her pregnancy was only just beginning to show and, on her trim, lithe body, it made her all the sexier.

Captain Swanson pushed his chair back and stood so fast, the chair rolled away and crashed into the wall. "I've got it!"

Andrei stared at the police captain. "Got what?"

"The answer to how you'll get inside the inn without arousing suspicion." The captain's mouth turned up at the corners. "You already know Hazel's daughter, Jocelyne, don't you?"

"I only met her yesterday when we discovered Angela's body." Andrei shook his head. "Why?"

The older man waved his hand as if encouraging Andrei to find the answer. "She's single, isn't she?"

"So?"

The police captain snorted. "Do I have to spell it out for you?"

"Please do."

A grin stretched across Swanson's face. "In order to get inside the inn without arousing suspicion, you can pretend to be Miss Baker's new boyfriend."

"Do what?"

The captain's grin slipped into a frown. "You heard me. You'll pretend to be Jocelyne Baker's boyfriend. That way you have every reason in the world to be at the inn…at all hours." A single brow rose over his eye. "Get my drift?"

Oh, he got it all too well. Andrei could already tell how the charade would go over with the independent Miss Baker. "Assuming she goes for this charade, it doesn't solve the fact that I'm a cop. With a police officer hanging around, the murderer will play it safe and avoid anything that draws attention to himself."

The captain's grin slipped and he scratched his chin for another minute, then his smile returned. "I have the solution to that problem as well."

"You do?" Even before his superior clued him in, Andrei's stomach twisted. "I get the feeling I'm not going to like this."

"Sure you will." Swanson rounded the desk and slapped his hand against Andrei's shoulder. "Seeing as you've been somewhat of a renegade, what with bringing all that Bronx attitude with you to our small town…you and I had a falling-out."

"I am? We did?" He knew he'd been a bear to get along with since his sister's death, but going against his captain? Okay, so maybe he had been in his face once or twice.

"That being the case, Officer Lagios…" Swanson rocked back on his heels, the corners of his mouth tipping upward. "You're fired."

"I'm what?" Andrei staggered backward and stared at his boss as though the older man had lost his mind. Even the thought of being fired made him burn all over.

"If you're going to spend time at the inn, it has to be solely on the basis of your relationship with the Baker woman, not as a cop." The captain spread his hands wide. "You're fired. Problem solved."

Andrei could see the idea had merit. Still, he'd never been fired from a job. "Unfortunately, you're making sense, and I'm not sure I like it."

"Don't worry. I'm not really going to fire you. But we have to make it look real enough the entire town buys it. You can't tell a soul, other than Jocelyne."

Andrei shook his head. "What about my family?" They wouldn't be happy.

"Especially not your family. It has to be convincing. We have to make it look like you and I had a major difference of opinion. We can't have the murderer thinking you're still on the payroll."

"I don't know." The thought of lying to his family didn't sit well with Andrei. They'd already been through so much because of him. Moving from the Bronx to Raven's Cliff had been his idea. Had they stayed in the Bronx, his sister would still be alive, not just another name on the growing list of the Seaside Strangler's victims.

"If you can think of another way to keep an eye on that inn and that plant, you let me know. In the meantime, you're fired. Turn in your weapon." The captain held out his hand.

"You're taking my gun?" The sinking feeling only got deeper as he handed over the gun to Swanson. His family would be devastated. They were counting on him to bring the

Seaside Strangler to justice. Getting fired from the police force would seem like he'd failed yet again.

"I know you have guns of your own. Now, make it look like you're upset. Yell a little, do something rash. I know you've wanted to throw something at me on more than one occasion." The captain placed a hand on his shoulder. "Trust me, Andrei, this is the only way."

"You're assuming a lot if you think Jocelyne Baker is going to just go along with this."

"You're good with the ladies. I'm sure you'll manage. Now, yell."

Andrei inhaled and let out a long breath. So be it. He drew in a deep breath and summoned all the anger he'd bottled inside over the senseless deaths of the young women thus far claimed by the Seaside Strangler and let it loose on a man he had nothing but respect for.

Captain Swanson handed him a wooden chair. "Go for it."

His breaths rasping in and out of his lungs, Andrei raised the chair and slammed it against the wall. *Let the games begin.* "You can't fire me! I quit!"

Chapter Five

At first she thought the odor might be something rotting on the shore nearby, but as the nasty smell grew stronger, permeating the air of Cliffside Inn, Jocelyne's sensitive nose wrinkled. With her stomach burbling and threatening to upend, she pushed away from her computer and descended the curved staircase to the first floor of the inn.

Having missed lunch, every one of her senses seemed on heightened alert, her olfactory nerves especially. When she rounded the corner to the expansive living area, a man dressed in rubber boots and wreaking of fish, bumped into her.

"Pardon me," he said, keeping his head down, barely meeting her gaze. An intense pair of bright blue eyes flashed up at her and back down again. He had to be around thirty, but the harsh weather and sun had leathered his skin and emphasized the fine lines at the corners of his eyes. Alex Gibson was one of her mother's boarders, a quiet solitary man who'd moved to Raven's Cliff during Jocelyne's long absence.

"Morning, Mr. Gibson. I'm looking for my mother. I don't suppose you've seen her?"

"No, no. I haven't." He moved around her as though he was in a hurry and didn't have time for casual conversation. As he rushed past, he darted a look back at her, his face reddening when he caught her staring.

Strange man. Somewhat attractive, but too reclusive. Dismissing Alex with a shake of her head, Jocelyne continued her search for her mother and the source of the stench.

"Mom?" Jocelyne wound her way through the elegant mansion, filled with antiques from a bygone era of opulence. Finding no sign of her mother in the meticulously clean modernized kitchen, she noted that the door to the cellar stood open, the stench wafting upward from the stairwell.

Jocelyne grabbed a paper towel and pressed it to her nose, fighting the rise of nausea, a band of annoyance tightening her gut. A tiny foot kicked the inside of her uterus in protest. With a hand pressed to the gentle swell of her belly, she moved down the steps into the basement. What was her mother up to now? "Mom?"

"Down here, dear," Hazel Baker called out.

As she descended into the basement, the thought that someone creepy had slipped down here to steal leaves from the henbane plant sent shivers of fear over her. What had once been an exciting place to play hide-and-seek now gave her the heebie-jeebies with images of spiderwebs, monsters and shadowy creatures taunting her healthy imagination. Not until she reached the bottom of the stairs did she remember to breathe.

In the far corner, the fluorescent lighting glowed over long tables lined with every kind of herb and plant imaginable. Her mother carefully cultivated the herbs for her homeopathic remedies to common ailments. Jocelyne was familiar with most of them, but she preferred to do her herb gardening in the outside greenhouse, not the basement. She'd inventoried her own plants, but she wasn't sure what her mother kept below the inn, besides the henbane.

The enormous old mansion had been converted to a boardinghouse and inn over a half century ago, with a low-ceiling basement running the full length. Floor joists and massive timbers held the rest of the three-story structure aloft, with the structural beams breaking up the space every sixteen feet.

Dried herbs hung from nails on beams, baskets littered the floor and shelves lined the walls. Everywhere she looked were plastic containers, leather pouches and ceramic pots filled with things even Jocelyne didn't dare to inquire about.

Her mother knew what was in each pot, pan, tub and sack. With the utmost care, she stored the herbs and ingredients she used in her decoctions for spells, potions and remedies.

"Back here. I'm in the middle of something." Across the floor, Hazel Baker's shimmering green-and-purple blouse and matching skirt reflected the light shining over an open book. Gold bangles dangled from her wrists, clinking with each movement of her arms and hands.

Her mother was most likely working on a potion or brew she planned to use on a member of the community, or worse, as a basis for a spell. Many of her vile-smelling concoctions managed to turn Jocelyne's stomach. Not a good thing for a pregnant woman.

As she fought the bile rising in her she wondered why she'd thought her mother might have changed. For over four decades, Hazel Baker had been a firm believer in all things Wicca, practicing the ancient pagan religion for the good of her body and her community, even if it cost her daughter dearly. Jocelyne sighed. "Remedy or potion?"

"Potion."

"Mom, I thought you said you'd quit making potions."

"I can't, honey." She glanced at the page in the book and then added ingredients to a cauldron of murky liquid, bubbling over a small gas stove, set against the wall. "Raven's Cliff needs me."

"Why?"

Hazel turned back to the ancient book, passed down to her by her mother, and lifted a yellowed page, laying it over gently. The *Book of Shadows* had been lovingly cared for by generations of women from her mother's family. "I know you don't like it when I practice my faith, but you have to understand." She gripped the corners of the book, her fingers turning white with the force, her normally happy face paling as she spoke. "There's evil here. I can feel it in my bones, in my skin, in the air I breathe." She faced her daughter, her dark-green eyes glowing with the intensity of her conviction.

A chill snaked across Jocelyne's skin and the muscles in the back of her neck tightened. She understood evil and bad omens. She'd been cursed with them for as long as she could remember. That didn't make it right to publicly acknowledge evil's existence. Nor to get everyone in town up in arms over something that might be nonexistent.

She shook her head from side to side. "Mom, there's evil everywhere, but there's also good. You shouldn't dwell on the bad." How many times had she told herself the same thing? Did she really adhere to her own words, or was it just lip service?

"I know, I know. But I can't let the evil continue to eat at the very foundation of Raven's Cliff. Too many horrible things have happened already."

"That doesn't mean you have to whip up something incredibly nauseating to cure what ails this community." Jocelyne pressed the paper towel to her nose and breathed, the stench finding its way through the layers of absorbent paper.

"I have to cure the curse."

"Mom, you're blowing this whole curse thing way out of proportion."

"Then how do you explain the Seaside Strangler? After the lighthouse burned, he struck that very next day, taking poor Rebecca Johnson. He tried to kill his second victim, but she got away before he could. Then he killed Cora McDonald and Sofia Lagios. All of them strangled with a seashell necklace."

The name hit Jocelyne full in the gut. "Did you say

Lagios?" She laid a hand on her mother's arm. "Was she any relation to Andrei Lagios?"

Her mother nodded, her eyes filling. "His little sister. She and her friend were murdered not too long ago on the night of their prom. Horrible tragedy."

So that explained Andrei's burning desire to catch the killer at all costs. Sorrow washed over Jocelyne, filling her chest with a deep ache. Andrei was still in mourning for his sister.

Being gone for ten years, she'd apparently missed more than the usual small town gossip.

"You see, I have to break this curse so that the town can finally live in peace."

"Mom, one potion won't cure a town of evil."

"I'm pulling out the strongest potions and spells in my *Book of Shadows*. I'll find the cure, if it's the last thing I do."

"Aren't you worried the townspeople will just make fun of you? You know what they think about your beliefs."

Her mother's brows dipped deeper. "And what do you think?"

Jocelyne held her tongue. She'd only been back a few days, back to mend fences and find resolution with her past. Her purpose was not to accuse her mother of being a nutcase ready for a one-way ticket to the loony bin with her very own monogrammed straitjacket. No matter what her mother believed or what she did, at her core, she meant well and strove to help others find peace and contentment.

Contentment. An elusive state Jocelyne had yet to achieve. She'd run away from Raven's Cliff in search of herself and peace of mind. That she was back spoke of her failure.

If Jocelyne had learned one thing in her hiatus from her hometown, she'd learned that when life took away everything, and you felt you had nothing left, you still had family. As if reminding her of the fact, a sharp pain jabbed her ribs. "I'll tell you what I think, Mom. I love you and I don't want to see you hurt."

She rounded the worktable and picked her way over a hefty bag of potting soil, tamping down all her frustrations long enough to wrap her arms around her mother. She seemed smaller and more fragile than Jocelyne remembered from ten years ago. The vibrant red hair she'd once worn loose and wild was streaked with gray and pulled into a neat chignon at the back of her head. Her once lovely face bore smudged brown age spots. When had her mother grown old? "Please, Mom, don't stir up trouble. I couldn't bear to see you laughed at."

Her mother pushed her to arm's length, her hands gripping her upper arms hard enough to bruise. "Honey, I don't give a rat's you-know-what who laughs at me. However, I do care about this town and the people who live here. I can't stand by and let the evil consume my home."

Jocelyne's belly tightened painfully. Drawing on her yoga training, she pulled in a deep breath and let it out slowly. "Okay. I know you have to do what you think is best." Extricating herself from her mother's grasp, Jocelyne stepped back, bumping into the bag of potting soil. "You're going to trip over that, if you're not careful."

Her mother smoothed her hands down her dress, her shaky chuckle warming the damp air. "I'll trip over it or you will?"

A smile twitched Jocelyne's lips. "Okay. I'll trip over it, if I'm not careful." She stared down at the bag. "Are you using potting soil in your potion?"

"Oh, no, sweetie." She shook her head. "Mr. Gibson brought it down the stairs for me just before you came down. I meant to tell him to stack it over by the grow lights, but my pot started to boil over about that time." She stirred the contents of the cauldron and sniffed the brew. "Helpful man. I hate to ask, but he doesn't seem to mind."

"Don't worry about it, I'll get it." Jocelyne bent to lift the bag, but when she tried, the muscles in her sides and back protested. Just another reminder that she was pregnant and unable to do things she normally had no problems with. "Sorry, Mom, no can do. It must weigh fifty or sixty pounds."

"That's why I asked Mr. Gibson to carry it down, dear. It was too bulky for me to maneuver down those narrow old steps."

"I'll see about getting someone to move it for you." In a minute or two. First she wanted to find out more about the comings and goings of the guests and employees of the inn. "Mom, who, besides you and Alex Gibson, comes down in this basement?"

"I'm the only one who comes down on a regular basis." She set the spoon on the stove top and switched the burner off.

"I know you do. But does anyone else ever come down?"

"Well, let's see." Her mother tipped her head to the side and tapped a finger to her chin. "Leah comes to the basement for the linens that go on the dining table. She also helps me with the cooking and occasionally comes down for pantry staples and spices." Her mother stared across the room at her. "Why do you ask?"

Jocelyne wasn't sure what she should tell her mother. What did she say? *The henbane plant in your basement might be the source of the drug used on the Seaside Strangler victims?* Jocelyne decided less was better. "Just curious. Do your guests ever come down?"

"Some do. Mr. Gibson delivered the potting soil today and has come down a time or two while I've been mixing remedies. He's quite interested in natural healing arts and learning more about Wicca. A veritable sponge of knowledge, that man. Other than him…I don't recall. My boarders have additional storage in the old stables out back. Don't worry. I keep my *Book of Shadows* locked in a chest when I'm not down here." She propped her fists on her hips. "Now, my turn. Tell me about the man Leah told me helped you with breakfast this morning."

"What do you know about Andrei?"

"Only that he's a nice young man. Are you two seeing each other?"

Jocelyne's face heated and she scrambled for a reason to escape. "I really should get back to my work. I have several orders to fill and mail out today."

"So it's okay for you to question me, but I can't question you?" Her mother's brows rose. "You like him, don't you?"

"He's bossy and entirely too…much of a man." Her face burned hotter. Now was the time to turn and run.

Her mother's quizzing look softened. "I'm glad he was there for you when you found Angela Wheeler." Her mother crossed to her and engulfed her in a hug. "I love you, Josie. Don't ever forget that. Now, go get something to eat. I won't have you starving my granddaughter."

Jocelyne blinked back tears, amazed at how emotional she'd been throughout her pregnancy. "How do you know it's a girl?"

Her mother turned back to her potion, casting a mysterious look over her shoulder. "I have my ways."

When Jocelyne reached the top of the basement stairs, Leah met her with a note in her hand. "There you are." She handed her the paper. "Andrei Lagios called while you were down there. He wants to meet you at The Cove Café at six."

A flood of heat thrilled through her system as she clasped the note in her hand. "Thanks, Leah."

"You two seeing each other?" Leah's brows waggled teasingly.

The thought sent butterflies skittering across her empty stomach followed quickly by frustration. For heaven's sake, she'd only just met the man. With nothing better to do in Raven's Cliff than gossip, the good people would have her and Andrei engaged by dinner. "Oh, no, we're just…" What were they? She didn't want to say that she was investigating the

Seaside Strangler with the man and have the employees and guests of Cliffside Inn run screaming. They weren't certain the strangler was even one of the guests or that he had indeed gotten the henbane from Hazel Baker's herb garden.

So how could she describe her relationship with Andrei Lagios? "We're just friends." And that's all it could ever be. She was six months pregnant and getting bigger by the day. Besides, she was poison in a relationship. She should have a sign hanging around her neck, *Fall In Love With Jocelyne Baker And Die*.

ANDREI SAT IN THE BOOTH at The Cove Café at a quarter of six, tapping his fingers against the shiny clean tabletop. Had she gotten his message?

"Top it off?" Dorothy Chapman, the owner of the diner, stood beside him, coffee carafe in hand, her blue eyes shining down at him.

"Please." He pushed the mug to the corner of the table.

"Waiting for someone?"

He might as well set the stage now. "As a matter of fact, I am." He smiled, but not too much, hoping it was enough to snow the woman. He was supposed to be there to see his girl. That part wasn't so hard to imagine. Jocelyne Baker wasn't what he'd call ugly. Her straight red hair fell like strands of silk over pale, peaches and cream skin. His mind could still conjure how she looked standing on the edge of the cliffs, the wind lifting strands of her hair and the hem of her white skirt.

Dorothy chuckled. "Must be someone special, by the look of you."

Andrei shot a glance at the older woman, his face heating. For a moment, he'd forgotten where he was and his jeans were disturbingly tight. Shifting in his seat to alleviate his discomfort, he reminded himself this was supposed to be an act. He'd have to be careful not to let it be anything else. Even if his soon-to-be partner in the game was a knockout, with a body that didn't quit, he couldn't afford to lose sight of his goal.

At that exact moment Jocelyne stepped through the door, her green eyes darting from tables to booths until they settled on him, a smile lifting the corners of her lips.

That smile hit him like a punch in the gut. She should smile more often. It made the entire room brighter.

"I'll be right back with another cup." Dorothy hurried off, casting a wink at Jocelyne as she went.

The redhead slipped into the booth across from Andrei. "What was that all about?"

Andrei pulled in a deep breath and leaned toward her. "I have a proposal."

Shock registered briefly in Jocelyne's eyes before her lips twisted into a crooked smile. "So soon? We only just met."

Wiping any humor from his face, he replied, "At the risk of sounding trite, I need an 'in' at Cliffside Inn, and you, Jocelyne Baker, have been nominated."

She shook her head, her brows dipping downward. "You're speaking in riddles."

Dorothy Chapman was on her way back with a coffee mug.

He grabbed Jocelyne's hand and leaned closer, forcing a smile while talking through his teeth. "Act like you're really happy to see me."

"What?" She tried to pull her hand away, but he held on tight while Mrs. Chapman set a mug in front of her.

"So, did you two meet in New York, or something?"

"N—" Andrei squeezed hard on Jocelyne's hand and she winced. "Ouch!"

"As a matter of fact, we did." He smiled across the table at Jocelyne just like a moonstruck teenager. "Actually at a little coffee shop on Fifth Avenue. Isn't that right, babe?"

For a second, she stared at him as if he'd lost his mind.

Then she smiled sweetly at Mrs. Chapman. "Yes, we did. I had a latte with cinnamon, he had a cappuccino. We shared a little table because it was so crowded and ended up talking until the shop closed." She laid her chin in her hand and batted her eyes at him. "It was so romantic."

The soft way she smiled and the twinkle in her emerald-green eyes had him forgetting his name. "Yes…yes, it was."

"That's so cute. And you both ended up here in Raven's Cliff. It never ceases to amaze me what a small world it is."

"Order up!" The cook called through the window to the kitchen. Dorothy smiled at them and left.

And none too soon. He wasn't sure he could remember what Jocelyne had said when she looked at him the way she was. She had his blood ricocheting off his eardrums and heating his body in all the wrong places.

When Dorothy was out of earshot, Jocelyne tugged at her hand. "Can I have my hand back?"

"Of course." Andrei sat straighter and willed his blood to slow in his veins.

When he let go, she rubbed at the red mark on her wrist. "So, what was all that about?"

"Our cover."

"What do you mean *our* cover? I'm a holistic healer and yoga instructor. We don't *do* cover. That's for cops and secret agents."

"You've just been recruited."

"I've been what?"

"Can you keep your voice down? You're going to blow our cover before we even get it established."

"I can't blow something that doesn't exist." She tempered her indignation by whispering. "Can you tell me what's going on?"

Andrei could kick himself. His libido was playing havoc with his brain, making him sound like a pushy cop. And the one thing he did know about Jocelyne was that she didn't ap-preciate pushy cops or pushy men. "I'm sorry. This isn't going like I planned." He shoved a hand through his hair and sighed. "It's possible that the Seaside Strangler has been drugging his victims with this henbane plant we found in your mother's basement, right?"

Her lips tightened. "So far, I'm with you."

"Makes sense to me that he's a frequent guest or boarder at the inn. Since we don't have anything to go on, I need to be on the inside at Cliffside Inn."

Dorothy Chapman walked by carrying a tray loaded with dinner for the table in the back corner.

Andrei leaned across the table and captured Jocelyne's hand again. "I need you, Jocelyne."

Jocelyne's fingers jerked beneath his. "For what?"

"I need a legitimate excuse to hang out at the inn and not alert the killer that we're on to him. If I had a girlfriend there, I'd have that excuse." He reached his other hand across, closing it around her one hand. "Will you be my girlfriend?"

Her eyes widened and she sucked in a breath. Then she let it out, shaking her head. "The killer will know you're a cop. How's that supposed to help?"

Andrei smiled. "I was fired today."

"You were what?"

"Look, I know this is a lot to take in, but I need to be on the inside, investigating the guests who have access to that plant. The captain has other cops conducting the interviews of potential suspects from your list and witnesses. For all intents and purposes, it'll appear as though I've had a difference of opinion with the captain, and I was canned."

Jocelyne stared at him for a long time, then sighed. "Okay, I'll do it. Anything to find the man who killed those women."

"Thanks. And keep the plan to yourself. That includes not telling your mother." Andrei finally let go of her hand and sat back.

"This means a lot to you."

Andrei's lips pressed together in a tight line. "Yes, it does."

"I'm in." She stood. "I have to get back to the house."

"Okay. And I don't want you walking outside alone." He tossed a couple dollars onto the table and followed her to the door. "You know we have to make this believable, don't you?"

"Yeah." She drew out the one word, her gaze swinging to his, her tongue darting out to wet her bottom lip. "What did you have in mind?"

"This." He let the glass door of the café close behind them, but while still in full view of the patrons inside and everyone hurrying home from work, he cupped the back of Jocelyne's head in the palm of his hand and leaned into her until his lips were a breath away from hers. "Don't look so surprised." Then his lips touched hers, pressing down.

Her mouth opened on a gasp.

As natural as breathing, his tongue slipped between her teeth and thrust against hers, tangling and tasting until they were both breathless.

"Get a room, will ya?" Mitch Chapman, one of the cops on the Raven's Cliff police force, eased by in a squad car, a grin stretched across his face.

Andrei's fingers trailed along the side of her cheek and brushed across her kiss-swollen lips. "I'm walking you home."

Chapter Six

All the way back to the inn, Jocelyne alternated between hot and cold flashes, and her breathing teetered on hyperventilation.

Andrei left her at the front door with the promise of seeing her bright and early the next morning.

When she had safely fallen through the front entrance of the inn without passing out cold, she closed the door and leaned against it, then sank to the floor.

Breathe in, breathe out.

What was she thinking? She couldn't agree to the arrangement Andrei had proposed. Not after that kiss.

That kiss.

Her face heated, her lips still on fire even after the brisk walk home in the cool air. Even her breasts tingled, her bra abrading her puckered, hypersensitive nipples. She crossed her arms over her chest and rocked forward, groaning. She couldn't fall for someone again. She couldn't risk having someone fall for her. Panic rose in her chest, leaving no room for oxygen.

Breathe in, breathe out.

She stopped midsway.

Andrei Lagios wasn't falling for her. Dating her was his cover. Only a cover. A good undercover cop could pretend to be almost anything. Even in love.

Jocelyne dragged in a deep breath and let it out in a slow steadying stream. *Just an act.* Her curse couldn't affect him if it was just an act. Only men who fell in love with her died.

The sooner they revealed the identity of the killer, the sooner the act would be over. Andrei would go back to the pretty blonde at the beauty shop and Jocelyne would give birth to her child. Alone.

"Are you all right, Ms. Baker?" The voice seemed to come out of nowhere.

Jocelyne stifled a scream.

Alex Gibson, dressed in clean blue jeans, a white cotton button-down shirt and an unzipped navy windbreaker stood in front of her.

Where had he come from? She hadn't heard footsteps or sensed someone else in the room. Her heart hammered against her ribs, reminding her she'd practically run all the way home from the diner in a lather over a kiss. A simple, fake kiss.

Schooling her face and voice to sound natural, Jocelyne stammered, "Yes, yes, Mr. Gibson, I'm all right." But she remained on the floor for fear her legs wouldn't hold her up.

He nodded, his gaze not meeting her eyes, instead dropping to where her hand rested on the ever-increasing bump of her belly. "Ms. Baker." His brows rose and his face flushed a ruddy red. "I didn't realize you were…well…here, let me help you up."

Despite her recent panic attack, she pulled herself together enough to force a smile for the poor man caught unawares by her "condition." "That's all right. I'm pregnant, not helpless." To prove it, she stood, unassisted. "See? I'm fine."

His face flushed even more. "Well, if you're sure you're okay, I'm late for my date with Lucy. I'd better go." He stepped around her and hurried out the door.

Note to self, next time you have another kiss-induced meltdown, make it to your room first.

Embarrassment stiffened her spine and gave her the strength to cross the floor, an idea springing to mind.

Rather than sit around and wait for the killer to reveal himself to her and Officer Lagios, she could take matters into her own hands. With a quick look around for other guests wandering her way, she hurried toward the stairs, taking them two at a time, her goal: her room and a change of clothing.

If she was going into the spy business, she'd better dress for the occasion. Spies needed to blend in with the environment. Wishing for an invisibility cloak, she settled for black slacks and a black turtleneck.

Once dressed, she stared at her bedroom door for a long moment, a plan forming. In order to investigate suspects, one had to gather information. Two of the long-term boarders at Cliffside Inn had just as much access to the basement herb garden as anyone. Grant Bridges and Alex Gibson.

From what she'd heard about Grant—care of Leah and her love of gossip—he could be a viable suspect. His fiancée disappeared on their wedding day, falling from the cliffs during the actual ceremony. So, he didn't have time to strangle her. Who was to say he didn't give her a little push? His room was on the second level of the old mansion. She could sneak in there and look for clues while he was out.

And who knew anything about Alex Gibson? He was a fisherman who dated the owner of Tidal Treasures, Lucy Tucker, and lived at Cliffside Inn. Other than those miniscule facts, he kept to himself, quiet and unassuming. Since he'd just left for the evening, she could start in his room.

All of Jocelyne's young life, her mother had drilled into her head that a guest's privacy was sacred. The thought of snooping through a guest's rooms while her mother's words echoed in her head gave Jocelyne a huge attack of guilt.

On the other side of that coin rested the prospect of being in close proximity to Andrei Lagios for an uncertain length of time, posing as his girlfriend. Anything to do with the sexy cop shook her so much, it outweighed guilt by a long shot.

Jocelyne brushed a speck of lint off her black slacks and smoothed the black turtleneck, the form-hugging jersey knit emphasizing her baby bump. Then, with a deep breath, she opened the door and went to work.

First, she needed keys and an excuse. She knew her mother kept the spare sets of keys inside a secret drawer in an antique commode cabinet in her suite of rooms on the main floor. Knowing her mother would be busy in the kitchen, cleaning up from the evening meal, Jocelyne sneaked into her bedroom and located the antique cabinet in the corner by the walk-in closet.

Now, where was that hidden switch she'd found when she was just a little girl? She opened a drawer and felt around inside until her fingers located the smooth wooden dowel. She pushed up and another drawer sprang open. The little thrill she used to get when she'd released the lock made her heart beat faster and a smile curl her lips.

Life as the town kook's only child hadn't been all bad. Her mother's free spirit combined with her love of antiques insured they had interesting furniture. Secret drawers, hidden panels, old pieces with a story were what Hazel had collected. Her favorites were gathered in her bedroom, from this old mahogany commode to the wardrobe standing against the wall with a hidden panel civil war soldiers used to hide guns and documents behind.

But for now, Jocelyne needed to get into Mr. Gibson's room while she could be relatively assured he wasn't there.

On the way back up to the second floor, she grabbed a stack of towels. Sounds of diners enjoying one of her mother's home-cooked meals carried through the large gathering room to the staircase that curved upward to the landing.

Armed with the spare set of keys and the stack of towels, Jocelyne hurried to the last room on the right. A quick glance over her shoulder assured her that no one else was in the hallway. She slipped the key into the lock, a wash of guilt making her fingers fumble. A door closed with a sharp click somewhere on the first floor.

Jocelyne shoved through Alex's door, closing and locking it behind her. Whew!

Breathe in, breathe out.

The baby kicked against her tight muscles, reminding her that she was pregnant and not in any shape to play spy. What had possessed her to think she was?

Now that she was here, she might as well see if there were any clues. Was mild-mannered fisherman Alex Gibson the Seaside Strangler? Would he have left any trace evidence of his dastardly deeds lying around in a room where the inn staff would come in and find it?

Probably not, but Jocelyne had to rule out one person at a time. Starting with Mr. Gibson.

She eased her way through the room, glad he'd left a bedside lamp on in the bedroom. Otherwise, she'd be feeling her way around in the dark. This suite had a bedroom, sitting room and separate bathroom. Alex had lived here for the past five years. Why get an apartment when you had an accomplished wait-staff to fix your meals and make your bed for you every day?

The room was surprisingly neat for a fisherman bachelor. Only a few items of clothing were left lying in the bathroom and by the fishy smell of them, there was a reason. A book of poetry lay on the nightstand with a bookmark sticking out of it.

Interesting. Jocelyne hadn't pegged Mr. Gibson as the poetry type. Actually she hadn't pegged him as anything. The man kept to himself, except for what her mother said was his weekly date with Lucy.

Jocelyne opened the wardrobe. This one was just a regular wardrobe, no special hidden panels for the man to hide a body in. Cotton shirts all in pale blue or white, hung neatly next to several pairs of clean blue jeans. One pair of loafers, a pair of hiking boots and a clean pair of mud boots stood in a neat row. Nothing stood out as a clue. How would she know if she was missing anything?

She turned toward the dresser. An unadorned wooden box rested on the smoothly polished cherrywood surface. Jewelry? She set the stack of towels on the bed and opened the box.

Inside was an antique sextant, a tool used by seafarers of old to find their way by the stars. Beside it was a sterling silver ring with a five-pointed star encased in a circle.

Jocelyne gasped and the ring dropped from her nerveless fingers, rattling against the wooden slats of the floor.

The pentagram was a symbol of the Wicca faith. Was Alex Gibson a Wicca believer?

Footsteps sounded in the hallway outside the bedroom door, pulling Jocelyne out of her stunned stupor. She stooped and grabbed the ring, setting it back in the wooden box.

The metal-on-metal click of a key turning in a lock sent her scrambling for a hiding place. She raced for the bathroom and jumped into the clawfoot tub, pulling the shower curtain around her as the apartment door swung open and someone stepped inside.

Jocelyne held her breath, willing the curtain to stop swaying.

Footsteps tapped across the wooden floors of the sitting room and into the bedroom. When they moved toward the bathroom, Jocelyne thought she'd have a heart attack.

Trust the baby to let her know about her attack of nerves. The tiny being inside kicked her as if it was running a personal marathon against her ribs. It was all she could do not to moan.

The noise stopped short of the bathroom and a clicking made it sound like something being locked. The tapping heels faded toward the apartment door. The door opened and closed.

Silence reigned for a full two minutes before Jocelyne allowed herself to move an inch. He'd come back to his room once, how could she be sure Mr. Gibson wouldn't come back again?

Moving the curtain to the side, she peered out. No Mr. Gibson. That was her cue to get the heck out. No more spying. She'd leave that to the professionals like Andrei Lagios.

Her breathing grew ragged again at just the thought of being in the same room with Officer Lagios.

As Jocelyne raced through the room, she noted the towels she'd left on the bed had been moved to the lounge chair.

So, he'd noticed the towels. He could possibly question her mother in the morning.

Well, let him. Jocelyne would just deny knowledge about anyone entering Mr. Gibson's room. But she'd have to figure out a way to ask her mother about Alex Gibson's Wicca ring. If anyone knew about a guest with any connection to the Wicca beliefs, her mother would. From what her mother said, Alex seemed interested in potions.

Jocelyne pressed her ear to the wood paneling of the door.

No sounds carried through the heavy lumber. For once, she wished the soundproofing in the old house wasn't nearly so effective.

She held her breath and eased the door open. The coast was clear. She gathered her wits and stepped out into the hallway, hurriedly closing and locking the door.

"Good evening, Ms. Baker."

The deep male voice made her jump. Had she been a cat, she'd have been clinging to the ceiling. She spun to face the other suspect, Grant Bridges.

"Oh, Mr. Bridges. I was just laying out fresh towels for Mr. Gibson. Would you like some, too?"

"No, thank you. Your mother placed fresh towels in my bathroom this morning."

Great, he'd caught her in the act of sneaking into another guest's room. So much for going into Bridges' room. He'd be suspicious of her now.

His eyes narrowed into slits. "Do you have any idea why I was called into the sheriff's office today for questioning in the Angela Wheeler murder?"

"Me?" Jocelyne squeaked, sure the heat in her face told it all. "N-no. Of course I don't have a clue." She squelched a groan. Wasn't she a poor excuse for Andrei's cover?

Grant's stare made her squirm until she forced a smile to her stiff lips. "Well, if you don't need anything, I hope you have a good evening." She edged past the man and headed for the staircase leading to her room on the upper floor. Once she reached the third-floor landing, she let out the breath she'd been holding and ran the rest of the way to her room.

It took an entire hour of meditation to bring her heart rate back to normal.

Tomorrow, she'd tell Andrei Lagios he could keep his spy mission. She wanted no part of it.

ANDREI PACED THE TILED FLOOR of his apartment deep into the night, regretting having kissed Jocelyne with every part of his being. Not only was he embroiling a pregnant woman in a dangerous operation, he'd found her lips entirely too soft and sensuous for his own peace of mind.

How the hell was he supposed to maintain focus on this case when the beautiful witch bedazzled him with her green-eyed gaze? With her well-toned muscles and the soft curve of her belly, she was perhaps the sexiest woman he'd ever met.

How he could feel that way about a pregnant woman was beyond him. He'd only known her a couple days, but he recognized the down-deep attraction growing in his gut. Every time he was around her, parts of his body hardened, the other parts softened until he didn't know whether he was coming or going.

What bothered him most about the entire situation was the knowledge that there was henbane in the basement of Cliffside Inn and someone had been using it to drug his victims. That someone had access to and could possibly be living at Cliffside Inn.

With the red-haired beauty, Jocelyne Baker. Would she be his next victim?

He blamed himself for the loss of his sister. If he'd caught the killer sooner, Sofia would still be alive, getting ready to go to college in New York City.

The killer would not add another victim to his growing list. And he certainly wouldn't add Jocelyne. She and her baby deserved a chance to live. And unlike Sofia, Jocelyne *would* live, if Andrei Lagios had anything to do with it.

Tomorrow he'd set the wheels in motion, put his plan in place and find out who was at the bottom of the murders.

Chapter Seven

Jocelyne spent the next day helping her mother with the cooking, cleaning and general operation of the rambling old inn. Anything to keep her mind off Andrei Lagios. He'd said he'd be by today, but it was already late afternoon and he hadn't set foot in the place.

Attacks of nerves, closely resembling panic, had her peering through the windows every time a car pulled up in the parking lot, or jumping when the front door to the inn opened and a guest walked in.

By the time six o'clock rolled around, Jocelyne, exhausted and past caring, flopped into a wingback chair positioned in front of the massive fireplace in the large gathering room. So much for worrying about what she'd say to the man about the whole investigation thing. He hadn't bothered showing up.

"What's wrong, dear?" Her mother settled onto the edge of a faded, floral Victorian sofa and leaned across to pat Jocelyne's knee. "You've been tense all day. Are you feeling well?"

What could she tell her mother and not spill the beans about the undercover operation? "I don't know. I'm just not myself today." She hadn't been herself since Andrei Lagios kissed her. At first she'd been shocked by her reaction. Now she was out of sorts, disgruntled by his failure to show and just plain cranky.

Her mother gave her one of those knowing smiles. "I'm sure he'll be by soon."

"Who? I'm not expecting anyone." Jocelyne couldn't remember saying anything to her mother about Andrei dropping by. How did she know?

"Oh, come on, don't play dumb with me." Her mother patted her knee again and then leaned back on the sofa, a grin spreading across her finely lined face. "You've been watching for someone all day. As jumpy as you are, it must be a man."

"I've been working all day," Jocelyne grumbled. "I haven't had time to look out the windows." The front door opened and Jocelyne's gaze shot to the person entering, her breath catching in her throat until she realized it was just Alex Gibson. Which reminded her...

"Right. You haven't been watching the windows or doors." Her mother gave an indelicate snort. "Is it that Lagios man from the police department? What time did he say he'd come?"

A sigh left Jocelyne's lungs. She couldn't lie to her mother, despite her desire to keep her feelings to herself. "He didn't say what time, just that he'd be by."

"Just like a man to leave a girl hanging. But don't you worry, he'll be here. He strikes me as honest and trustworthy."

Even though she wanted to wallow in her anger and self-pity, Jocelyne couldn't help the smile curving the corners of her lips. "You make him sound like a bassett hound."

"Your father was like that." Hazel's green eyes misted as she stared into the glowing flames.

Jocelyne chuckled. "Like a dog? That doesn't sound very attractive."

"Oh, not the dog part, but he was very honest and trust-worthy."

Settling back in her chair, Jocelyne asked, "What else was he like, Mom? Tell me about Dad." Her mother rarely spoke of her father and she'd felt like she'd missed a big part of her life because of it. He'd died when Jocelyne was three, hardly old enough to remember.

"He was tall, handsome and so very strong, with a twinkle in his eyes like he knew the punch line of every joke. He was born and raised a fisherman here in Raven's Cliff. I was the outsider. We met when he was in the navy outside of Norfolk, Virginia."

Her mother smiled. "I didn't believe in love at first sight. Until I met your father. He brought me to his home and bought the old inn for me so that I would never be alone while he was out to sea. He worked hard to make the payments by bringing in extra catches. There were times I thought he loved his mistress the sea more than me." Her mother stared down at her hands clasped together in her lap. "In the end, she claimed him." She looked up, her liquid green gaze capturing Jocelyne's. "He was the love of my life. Sometimes I miss him so much it hurts."

A knot formed in Jocelyne's throat. All those years of wishing her mother wasn't such a flake seemed unimportant. Her mother had struggled through life without the man she loved, raising a daughter who had shown her more hate than anything else. How difficult it must have been for her.

"I'm sorry, Mom."

Her mother's green eyes widened. "Goodness, dear, whatever for?"

"For being such a brat." She rose from the chair and sat beside her mother, wrapping an arm around her shoulders. "I love you."

"I love you, too, dear." Hazel Baker stroked the back of Jocelyne's head, like she had when Jocelyne was a little girl. "And I care about this town that your father loved so dearly. I'd do anything to break that blessed curse."

Jocelyne stiffened and pulled away. "Mom, what did you do with that potion you were brewing in the basement?"

"I'm letting it steep, honey. Tomorrow's a full moon, did

you realize that?" The grandfather clock in the corner chimed, and Hazel Baker leaped to her feet. "Oh dear, look at the time. I really must get back to dinner setup."

"Mom?" Jocelyne rose as well and glanced around at the empty room before asking in a low tone, "What do you know about Grant Bridges and Alex Gibson?"

"They both board here at the inn." Her mother's brows drew inward.

"I mean what else do you know about them?"

"Mr. Bridges, bless his heart, lost his fiancée on the day of their wedding. She fell off the cliff. Poor soul. In her wedding dress, on her wedding day. She was never found. The sea claimed her as well." Hazel Baker shook her head staring off into space. "Mr. Bridges had given up his apartment to move in with Camille after the wedding. When she disappeared, he had nowhere else to go but here."

"What about Alex Gibson?"

A smile replaced the frown on her mother's face. "Mr. Gibson? Oh, he's such a nice man. He's always helpful and he loves this town even though he didn't grow up here. He and I get along just fine, both of us being Wiccan."

Jocelyne tipped her head. "How did you know he was Wiccan?"

"I was cleaning his room one day and found a ring with a pentagram on it. I asked him about it."

"And he told you?"

"Just because he's a recluse doesn't mean he's without religion, dear." Her mother brushed the front of her apron. "I know you don't like the fact that I'm Wiccan, but it's who I am. Your father knew it when he married me, and it didn't make a difference."

A pang of longing tugged at Jocelyne's heart. Why couldn't everyone be like her father? "Doesn't it bother you that the people of Raven's Cliff never really accepted you?"

"I don't hold that against them, dear. I just want peace and happiness for the town your father loved."

"Don't you find it odd that Alex Gibson is Wiccan?"

"It would explain why he's such a recluse. Good thing he has Lucy to keep him from being too much of a hermit. What did you want to know about him?"

"Nothing. I was just curious about the boarders here."

"Well, I'd love to stay and chat a while, but you know how it is when you run an inn. I have to get back to the kitchen or I'll have hungry people yelling because dinner's late." She leaned across and bussed Jocelyne's cheek then looked over her shoulder and smiled. "Looks like your man is finally here."

Jocelyne's stomach flip-flopped and she steeled herself to act normal when she turned.

Andrei stood framed in the front entrance, the sun shining behind him casting his face in shadows.

No matter how hard she willed herself to act like his presence meant nothing, Jocelyne's face heated, her lips tingled and her breath grew more ragged. "So, you're here." Of all the stupid, inane comments she could have come up with, she couldn't have chosen better.

"I'm sorry I didn't call sooner. I had to empty my office."

"Andrei Lagios, so glad you could come by. Can I get you a cup of coffee and some scones?" Jocelyne's mother hurried over and extended her hand in welcome, while her daughter stood rooted to the floor, unable to move an inch on her rubber legs.

"No, thank you, Mrs. Baker."

Hazel shook his hand and then let go of the hand but not his comment. "What's this about emptying your office?"

Andrei moved farther into the great room, closing the door behind him. His gaze was zeroed in on Jocelyne's face.

"Captain Swanson and I had a difference of opinion." His mouth pressed into a straight line. "His opinion counted more than mine. I was fired."

"Oh dear, that's such a shame. Such a terrible shame." Hazel Baker's brows drew into a frown. "Does it have to do with Angela Wheeler's murder?"

"You could say that."

"All because of that blasted curse." The older woman wrung her hands. "If only the Sterling boy hadn't neglected the lighthouse, none of this would be happening."

"Well, what's done is done. I'm unemployed and looking for work."

"That's right. You are. I suppose I could use a handyman around here since Jason Jones moved to Bangor. But not on a permanent basis. Just job by job. The gutters on the west side of the inn have come loose, do you think you could help me out?"

The thought of Andrei Lagios working for her mother sent Jocelyne scurrying across the floor to intervene. "Mom, I'm sure he needs to find permanent employment somewhere."

Hazel gazed up at Andrei. "I can't offer you permanent employment, but if you need work in the interim, I have a list I've been meaning to get to."

Andrei stared across at Jocelyne, his mouth turning up into a grin. "I'd be happy to help out. Is tomorrow soon enough?"

"Of course. I'll expect you here at eight in the morning." Her mother smiled. "Good, that's settled. Now I must get to dinner. Will you be staying, Andrei?"

"No, I was hoping to talk Jocelyne into going out to supper with me."

"Oh, well, I'm sure she'd love to."

"Mom, I can speak for myself. Why don't you go cook something?"

Her mother's eyes twinkled. "I get it. I'll leave you two lovebirds alone. See you tomorrow, Andrei." With a swish of her deep-green skirt, she left her daughter swirling in her wake.

Jocelyne loved her mother, but sometimes the woman drove her nuts.

ANDREI COULDN'T SUPPRESS the chuckle rising up in his throat. The look of helplessness on Jocelyne's face was priceless.

"What do you find so funny? I have to live with her." The anger didn't quite reach her eyes. She smacked her hand against his chest and he captured it in his.

"Lovebirds?" A gentle tug brought her up against him. "Isn't that what we're supposed to be?"

Her peaches and cream complexion darkened into a rosy shade of pink. "I can't do this," she whispered.

"Why not?" He brushed a stray strand of deep-red hair from her face. "Am I that ugly you can't see yourself with me? Even for an undercover operation?"

"Andrei Lagios...ugly?" She gave him an unladylike snort. "Be serious. You know you're every woman's dream."

"Is that so? Am I yours?" He tipped her chin with a large calloused finger, liking that he had her off balance. Liking more, the way her warm lithe body fit against him. Hell, liking it way too much. "Don't answer that."

"Afraid it won't be the answer you want?"

"Maybe." And afraid of the way her full lower lip looked like ripe fruit ready to taste. Or the heat of her body might make him want more than a taste. "Maybe I'm afraid of you."

She rolled her eyes. "That'll be the day."

Rein it in, man, before you start liking her too much. He suspected he might be a little late for that. Still, he set her back far enough away to look her over. "You'll do for what I had in mind."

"I'll do?" Jocelyne grimaced. "Was that a backhanded compliment? Or should I be insulted?"

Grabbing her hand, he turned toward the kitchen. "First, let's find out if anyone else is here to see us together and then I have a surprise for you."

"Surprise?" She let him drag her several steps toward the sitting room before she dug her heels into the floor. "Hey, don't change the subject. You didn't answer me. What do you mean, 'I'll do'?"

"Your dress. It's nice." He tugged her toward the dining room. As soon as they crossed into the dining room, Andrei pulled her into the curve of his arm and waved at Leah Toler waiting on the tourists who'd arrived in time to enjoy the fall foliage before the weather turned nasty. "Hello, Leah." Nodding at the strangers, he called out, "Good evening." He landed a playful kiss on top of Jocelyne's head, inhaling the flowery scent of her shampoo. His groin tightened. Yeah, he could like this little charade a bit too much, if he let himself.

Andrei leaned through the swinging doors and shouted, "We'll be back late, Mrs. Baker. Hope you don't mind."

"Not a problem. Take care of my little girl." Hazel Baker waved one hand while the other stirred whatever smelled so good in the huge stockpot.

"Yes, ma'am." He grinned and practically dragged Jocelyne all the way back through the inn and out into his waiting car.

"Where are we going?" Jocelyne buckled her seat belt below her belly and stared straight forward, refusing to turn and look at Andrei.

He paused with his fingers on the keys. "Are you mad or something?"

"No." Her voice was short, crisp and definitely irritated. She looked more flustered than angry.

Andrei suppressed a grin, enjoying her discombobulation. He turned the key and the car roared to life. "You're mad."

"Not mad, but concerned." Her hand fluttered and she

heaved a big sigh. "This is all happening so fast. I don't know if I can do this."

"You don't have to do anything but let me be your man for a few days." As he backed out of the parking lot, he cast a glance in her direction. "In fact, I'd rather you didn't do anything but act as though you like me. Don't get involved in the investigation, other than that." He braked to a halt and reached out to tip her chin toward him. "Promise?"

When her gaze didn't meet his, his heart stuttered. "You haven't done anything you'd like to tell me about, have you?"

She pulled her chin from his fingers and looked out the front windshield, her face flushing a pretty shade of pink. "I did."

Andrei sucked in a breath and eased it out, then in slow, deliberate tones, he asked, "What did you do?" Anger, fired by fear for her life, made his tone a little more hard-edged than he'd intended. But if it made her take notice, all the better.

She gazed at him, her mouth twisting into a hesitant half smile. "I may have sneaked into Alex Gibson's room and had a look around."

"May have?" Andrei slammed the shift into Park and then turned and grabbed Jocelyne's arms, his heart slamming against his ribs as if he'd been in a flat-out run since he'd arrived at the inn. "Did Gibson see you?"

"No, he had gone out on a date." Her gaze dipped below his. "At least I thought he'd left."

"You mean he came back?" Andrei's voice rose, tension knotting in his gut.

"I think it was him. I don't know, I was hiding in the bathtub. I couldn't see anything through the shower curtain." She looked up at him. "Why are you yelling at me?"

"Did anyone see you entering or leaving his room?"

Her lips pressed into a tight line. "Yes. Grant Bridges caught me coming out."

"Did you talk to him, did he say anything?"

"I told him I was leaving fresh towels for Mr. Gibson and asked him if he wanted some." Her face reddened. She wasn't telling him everything.

"Anything else happen?"

Jocelyne stared at her hands. "Not much."

"Let me be the judge," Andrei said.

"He asked if I knew why the sheriff called him in for an interview. I told him no."

"And did you turn as red as you are now?"

She threw her hands in the air. "I can't help it, I turn red when I'm tense!"

Andrei squeezed his eyes shut and counted to five, breathing in and out slowly. When he opened his eyes, he pinned her with his stare. "Understand this. I only want you to play the part of my cover. You are under no circumstances to question, snoop around or spy on the suspects. Any one of the men who frequent the inn could be the Seaside Strangler."

"I only wanted to help." She stared down at where his hands still gripped her arms. "You're hurting me."

Andrei immediately let go and transferred his iron grip to the steering wheel. He continued, holding his voice and emotions in check by a very thin thread, "Jocelyne, he's killed four women so far. He won't hesitate to kill a fifth." He glanced over at her, not just seeing Jocelyne Baker, but Cora McDonald, Rebecca Johnson, Angela Wheeler and his sister, Sofia. "Don't be the fifth."

Jocelyne rubbed her arms where his fingers had been and for a long moment the silence stretched between them. Then she reached out a hand and laid it on his arm. "I'm not going to die, Andrei. I have a baby to think about. I won't do anything that could put my baby in danger."

"You just did." Andrei shifted into Drive and pulled out onto Main Street. He didn't know what else to say. The earlier easy camaraderie had vanished. In its place was strained silence and he didn't know how to break it, nor did he want to. What Jocelyne had done scared the mud out of him. If the killer clued in that she and Andrei were investigating the case, he might make her his next target.

His chest tightened and his knuckles turned white on the steering wheel. Misty fog crept over the landscape, at first softening the edges of the buildings and then muting them altogether. Andrei switched his headlights from bright to dim to avoid the blinding glare off the encroaching haze.

"You said you had a surprise for me." Jocelyne's attempt at a bright tone faded into the darkening interior of the car. "What is it?"

All the anticipation of taking Jocelyne out faded in comparison with the fear that thudded against his chest at her brazen attempt at sleuthing. "We're going to the Seafarer's Bounty for dinner," he replied, his voice flat.

"What?" She glanced down at her casual skirt and pumps and a hand rose to her hair. "You could have warned me we were going somewhere fancy."

"I only just got the word. I was going to take you to my parents' house, that's where I really was today. But Captain Swanson informed me Mayor Wells, his assistant, Rick Simpson, and Grant Bridges were meeting for dinner tonight."

"And this has *what* to do with us?"

"No time like the present to make our little romance public, especially in front of three of our potential suspects."

"You really think the mayor and his assistant are possible suspects?"

"They spend time at Cliffside Inn, don't they?"

"Yes, but…"

"Then they're suspects, just like Alex Gibson and any other male who frequents the inn and has access to the henbane plant."

A shiver shook Jocelyne's narrow frame. "I couldn't sleep all last night."

An image of her lying in bed in a silky nightgown wasn't any way to keep his mind focused on an investigation. No, sir. He'd have to steer away from those mental pictures. A cat darted out into the street and Andrei swerved to miss it.

Jocelyne swayed, her shoulder brushing against his. An electric shock pulsed through him. This charade wasn't going to be easy. He couldn't think straight when she was around. He couldn't concentrate on the investigation when he worried more about her and her unborn child. "Did the baby keep you awake?"

"Are you kidding? Just knowing a killer might be one of the people who live in the same house as I do had me tossing and turning until the wee hours."

"I don't like it." He'd thought about that until after midnight and sleep had eluded him as well. "I'm moving in with you until this is all over." Whoa, where had that come from? Was he out of his mind?

Jocelyne stared at him as if he'd grown an extra ear or eye. "You can't move in with me."

Moving in with Jocelyne made sense the more he thought about it. "Why not? By the end of this evening, everyone in Raven's Cliff will think we're sleeping together. Why not make it true?"

"Because, I'm not sleeping with you, that's why." She shook her head. "I can't believe you even suggested it."

His teeth ground together. "I'd rather know you were safe than care what the townspeople think."

"But I care."

"Do you think your mother would have a problem if I moved in?" He tapped his finger on the steering wheel and stared out at the road ahead, already planning his move.

Jocelyne rolled her eyes. "Yes."

"Why? It's the perfect solution. I'll move into the inn.

That way, I can make sure you're safe and do all the looking around I need." Andrei glanced over at her, a smile playing at the corners of his lips. "I could stay in a different room, if it makes you feel better."

She stared into the fog, her chest rising and falling faster than normal. "If you're living in the inn, we don't need to act like we're lovers." She crossed her arms over her belly. "Which is just as well, I don't know how we'd keep up the pretense for any length of time."

"It's too late. Leah's been known to gossip. Half of Raven's Cliff will know by midnight. The other half will know after we eat dinner at the Seafarer's Bounty. Besides, we're here, and I'm hungry."

Lights glowed like hazy yellow circles on the corners of the Seafarer's Bounty. The sprawling white restaurant, built in the shape of a fishing boat, happened to be the most exclusive eating establishment in Raven's Cliff.

"How did you get a reservation on such short notice?"

Andrei smiled. "It may surprise you to know…I have friends."

"That does surprise me. I thought everyone hated cops."

"I'm one of the recently unemployed cops. Remember?" He shifted into Park and pulled the keys from the ignition. "You can stop hating me now."

"No, I can't," she muttered.

Her voice barely carried over the road noise of the car. Andrei had to strain to catch her words, but he caught them. "Afraid you'll like me too much?" He climbed out of the car and strode around to the other side.

Jocelyne had the door open before he got there. "Did anyone ever tell you that you're very full of yourself?"

"More than once." He held out his hand, refusing to get out of her way until she placed her hand in his and let him pull her to her feet.

They entered the restaurant and were immediately seated at a table in the corner, within clear view of Mayor Wells, Rick Simpson and Grant Bridges.

Bridges glared at Jocelyne from the moment she stepped through the door.

Andrei maneuvered his body to block the other man's view, not liking the malevolent look the district attorney leveled on his "date."

As they were seated, Jocelyne leaned across and rested her hand on Andrei's.

His pulse quickened and he fought back the urge to draw her into his arms.

She leaned close and gave him a heart-stopping smile, her green eyes sparkling in the candlelight. "I'm picking up half the check."

He lifted her fingers to his lips and pressed a kiss to each, one at a time. "No…you're…not." Then he rolled her hand over and pressed his mouth to her palm.

The more he kissed, the wider her eyes grew. "Oh, you're gooood." What started out with a sarcastic sting, drifted into a soft and breathless sigh.

Good, he was getting to her. "Honey, you haven't seen anything yet. I bet if I wanted to, I could convince everyone in this room that I love you."

Jocelyne gasped, jerked her hand free of his and tucked it in her lap.

He expected sarcasm or some flip remark, but her gasp made him wonder what nerve he'd struck.

The waitress arrived at just that moment and Andrei cringed. *Oh, please. Not now, damn it.*

Briana Rogers, dressed in the uniform of the waitresses at the Seafarer's Bounty, a simple black skirt and white blouse, smiled and threw her arms around his neck. "Andrei, it's been forever since you came in here last." Her hug went on so long he could feel the heat rising up his neck into his cheeks. "Why haven't you come by to see me? This place gets so boring."

When Briana pulled back, she blinked at Jocelyne. "Oh, I'm sorry, I didn't see you there."

"Obviously," Jocelyne muttered beneath her breath, yet loud enough for the sarcasm to come across.

Briana took their orders and scurried back to the kitchen to deliver them to the cook. But even after she'd gone, the teasing mood didn't return.

"Let's get something straight." Jocelyne's expression was sober, emotionless. "This is all an act. Even if either of us wanted to, and I'm not saying I do, there can never be anything between us."

His lips curled upward. "Do I detect an attempt at setting rules?"

"You're damn right." She leaned closer, her breasts pressed against the table, a fake smile plastered across her pretty lips. "There will be no relationship between the two of us other than the bogus one for this investigation. Understand?"

Not that he planned on anything happening between them, but damned if he hadn't felt a spark of something for this spicy woman with the deep-red hair and mysterious green eyes. A spark of something very much like admiration, heavily laced with lust.

"Tell me you understand the rule." The pleading quality of her voice spoke to something more than anger over a flirting waitress. An emotion that went a lot deeper and actually scared Jocelyne Baker.

Something he'd said or done had scared her and she threw rules at him to protect herself.

But one thing Andrei had never been good at was following the rules.

"I understand perfectly," he replied.

He understood rules were meant to be broken. He looked forward to breaking a few with the lovely Jocelyne.

Chapter Eight

"If you'll excuse me, I need to go to the bathroom." Jocelyne stood so fast, her chair teetered, before its legs fell back to the floor. "You know…baby…bladder. I'll be back." She practically ran from the room, her bladder only being a fraction of the problem. The challenging gleam in Andrei's eyes and her own inability to keep her distance mentally and physically from the man caused her even greater concern.

In the ladies' restroom, she quickly relieved herself. As if sensing her distress, the baby kicked and rolled across her belly like it was using her ribcage as monkey bars.

Jocelyne washed her hands and splashed water on her heated cheeks.

What was she thinking getting involved in any way whatsoever with a man like Andrei Lagios? A man she could fall in love with? Her track record wasn't good. It was absolutely frightening. If by some miracle Andrei fell in love with her, too, he'd be dead within weeks.

Too?

She stared at her reflection, pressing her hands to her cheeks. Was she falling in love with the man? How could she? She'd known him all of three days. She'd known her fiancé longer than that before she'd considered using the *L* word with him. And her first love out of college she'd dated for six months before she felt anything deeper than lust. For that matter, lust was a very powerful emotion.

That was it. Her hands dropped to her side. She was in lust with the sexy cop. Who wouldn't be? The man was constructed like a male bodybuilder with shoulders stretching impossibly wide, skin pulled tight over well-defined muscles, a narrow waist and the perfect butt.

Her hands rose to her flaming cheeks. Yeah, it was lust.

As long as she recognized it as such and kept him at arm's length, he'd be all right. Under no circumstances would she encourage him to fall in love with her. Under no circumstances could she let her own desires override his safety.

Pep talk complete, Jocelyne left the ladies' restroom.

A door at the end of the short hallway closed behind what looked like Mayor Wells. Was he leaving already? If that was the case, she didn't have to keep up the self-destructive pretense of being with Andrei Lagios. They could actually relax and enjoy their meal.

Curious, Jocelyne walked to the end of the hallway and eased the exit door open. On well-oiled hinges, it didn't make a sound.

This made it easier to hear the rumbling of voices in the dense fog.

Jocelyne couldn't make out the words, but they sounded angry. A loud thump, followed by a grunt and moaning, had Jocelyne's heart in her throat. Someone was hurt.

Without thinking, she left the safety of the back door and stepped off the back porch. The fog immediately enveloped her. If not for the glow of the light over the exit, the restaurant would have disappeared.

She tiptoed in the direction of the sounds, careful not to bump into anything that could hurt her baby.

A deep gravelly voice echoed in the gloom. "Count this as a warning." Another thump and sharp grunt was followed by a moan. "Tell anyone about this and we'll make you hurt even more. Take it to the cops and you're a dead man." Footsteps clicked against the pavement, headed her direction.

Jocelyne turned in what she thought was the direction of the restaurant, but the glowing lights had melted into the mist. A faded glow reflected off millions of tiny droplets of mist, and she could no longer tell which direction it came from. Where the hell was she? She ran a couple steps, fear washing over her, spurring her on.

"What's that?" The gravelly voice sounded close by.

"Someone's out here," a smoother, deeper voice responded. "Take care of it."

The ominous words struck terror in her heart. She turned first one way and then another. Which way? A glance over her shoulder revealed two dark faceless shapes looming out of the mist.

"There!" The footsteps sped up, until they pounded against the gravel.

Jocelyne swerved left and ran in the opposite direction, unwilling to find out what they'd do if they caught her, determined not to give them the chance. In her dash for a place to hide, she bumped into a trash can, knocking it over. She smothered a curse as pain radiated out from her hip. Barely slowing, she kept moving forward, leaping over the spilled garbage.

"Over there!" the gravelly voice shouted.

Her heart slamming into her ribs, Jocelyne found a wall behind the trash can and followed it to the right, hopefully back toward the door she'd left the restaurant through. Moving as quickly as she could in the murky dark, she ran in a half-crouch, watching her every step to avoid further noisy encounters. She moved so fast she almost walked off the end of the pavement. Teetering on the edge of a sharp drop-off down a rocky cliff, she stifled a scream. She couldn't go any farther forward and she couldn't go back in the direction she'd come.

She'd been a fool to come out in the fog to begin with. She was pregnant for heaven's sake. Had she lost all common sense?

Footsteps neared her location and she hunkered low, trying to blend into the fog, the pavement and the rocks dropping off behind her.

"See anything?" gravel-voice whispered.

"Not a damn thing," Mr. Smooth replied.

"Got to be here somewhere."

A shoe slipped in loose gravel not far from where Jocelyne crouched.

Her pulse pounded against her eardrums so loudly, she thought surely they'd hear it. For the longest time, she held her breath, afraid even the sound of her breathing would carry to the shadowy thugs. They were so close, the scent of stale cigarettes wafted toward Jocelyne's position.

She tensed her muscles and allowed herself to inhale silently. *Breathe in, breathe out.*

Balanced on her toes, she prepared to spring past the two headed her way. She braced her fingers on the ground like a runner at the starting block.

The baby gave her a reassuring kick that it, too, was ready to make a move.

Darker shadows swayed in the mist, forming above her. It was now or never.

"Jocelyne?"

When Andrei's voice pierced the heavy fog shattering the silence, Jocelyne almost collapsed with relief. But it wasn't over yet. Two men still lurked in the darkness and she hadn't found her way back into the restaurant. She couldn't call out a response to Andrei and risk the men finding both her and Andrei. She had to remain quiet long enough for the men to leave.

"Mayor Wells! What happened?" Andrei muttered a curse.

On the edge of the pavement, with nothing but a rocky

drop-off behind her and two men groping around the darkness in front of her, Jocelyne strained to see through the fog, concentrating on every little sound above the gentle swish of a calm sea against the rocky shore. Were those footsteps hurrying away? Was that loose gravel ground beneath a leather sole?

A car door slammed a distance away and an engine revved, filling the silence with its mechanical roar.

"I'm all right, damn it. Leave me alone."

"No can do, sir. You're hurt. Let me help you up."

A grunt was followed by a string of curses. "Damn muggers."

"Did you see who it was? Can you describe your attackers?"

"Hell, no. They hit me from behind."

Jocelyne's knees shook as she walked toward the voices, dodging around the trash can she'd knocked over a moment before. Every sway in the fog, every deepening shadow made her jump. When two dark shapes appeared before her, she froze. "Andrei?" she said, her voice barely above a whisper.

"Jocelyne!" The taller form lurched toward her. Andrei materialized in front of her and she fell against his chest, never happier to see a man than she was to see him.

He folded her into his arms and held her tight. "You're shaking, babe. Where have you been? I was getting worried."

The mayor limped within view, a dark bruise forming on his jaw and a cut oozing blood from his right cheekbone. "How long have you been out here?"

Instinct made her lie. "I just stepped out for a breath of fresh air and immediately got lost in the fog." She stared at the older man in the limited light from the back porch. "What happened to you, Mayor Wells?"

He brushed at his suit lapel. "Muggers."

"That's awful!" Jocelyne would bet her entire stock of herbal remedies the man was lying. Hell, she knew he was. Anger surged in her and she pushed away from Andrei, digging in her purse for her cell phone. "I'll call 911. The police should know about this immediately." With a flip she had it opened and her finger on the way to pressing the speed dial button for emergency services. She'd call his bluff, just to see how far he would take the lie.

"No need," Mayor Wells insisted. "Lagios, here, can tell them."

"As a matter of fact, I no longer work for the Raven's Cliff Police Department. I was laid off today." He nodded toward Jocelyne. "Make that call, babe. The attack should be investigated."

Warmth pushed against the cold fear she'd experienced only moments before. It was as if Andrei had read her mind and he, too, was calling the mayor's bluff.

Jocelyne pressed speed dial for 911 and hit Send.

"No!" The mayor reached out and snatched Jocelyne's phone, snapping it shut before he handed it back to her. "I don't want to file a report. I'll have a word with the police captain in the morning. I'd rather not have the attack on public record. It's bad for business. Now, if you'll excuse me, I was having dinner." He straightened his jacket and strode none too steadily, toward the glow of lights over the back door.

When the door clicked shut behind him, Jocelyne let out a breath she hadn't realized she'd been holding. "He was lying."

"I figured as much." Andrei drew her against him. "What the hell were you doing out here in the first place?"

"I saw Mayor Wells leave through the rear exit. I was curious where he was going and why he'd sneak out the back, so I followed."

Hard as she tried, she couldn't keep her body from shaking as her remembered fear washed over her like a tidal wave. "I heard sounds like someone being hit and I figured it might be the mayor. When I heard two voices talking and neither sounded like Wells, I figured they outnumbered him. I was worried about him so I followed the sounds." Her body trembled and she couldn't stop it once it started. She shook so hard her teeth rattled. "I had to check on the mayor."

Andrei opened his jacket and tucked her inside, wrapping his arms around her, holding her against the warmth of his body. "You shouldn't have left the restaurant at all. Haven't you heard a word I've said? It's not safe."

"I know, I know. It was stupid of me, but I had to stop them. They might have killed the mayor."

He stroked her hair and down her back to her waist. "Did you get a look at their faces?"

"In this soup, I couldn't see anything. Nothing. But one of the men said, 'Take this as a warning,' as he hit the mayor. But get this, he followed up with, 'Take it to the police and you're a dead man.'"

"I'll inform the captain. This might have something to do with the trouble the mayor's been in lately with kickbacks on drug deals."

"The mayor?" Jocelyne clutched the front of Andrei's shirt. "And he's still in office?"

"Go figure. I get the feeling he's only there because no one else wants the job. Do you feel like eating or do you want to go home?"

She breathed in the scent of Andrei's aftershave. The shaking had stopped and she wasn't as cold as a few moments ago. Mostly because in Andrei's arms she felt safe.

His hands smoothed over her hair again, and was that a kiss she felt skim her temple?

Heat seared a path into her belly and lower. Her breath caught and held. *No. This can't happen.* But she wanted to stay right where she was, in the circle of his arms. Safe and secure.

She could come to rely on him too much. And she couldn't

let him get any closer than a professional basis. With her breasts pressed against his chest and only a thin layer of clothing between them, she'd consider that closer than a professional basis.

With a last deep breath, she stiffened her backbone and pushed away. "We have to go back inside and act like nothing happened, or there'll be more talk than we want at this point." She turned to follow Mayor Wells back toward the twin circles of light over the door she'd lost sight of minutes before. Had it only been a few minutes?

For Jocelyne it had been a lifetime. Her energy drained, she forced herself to walk down the hallway. Stopping in front of the ladies' bathroom, she almost laughed. This is where the evening's excitement had begun. "I'm going to wash my hands, then we're going to sit down to a pleasant meal. My baby needs nourishment." Although eating was the last thing on her mind.

"I'll wait here for you."

She smiled at him, that warm feeling welling in her chest. "Thanks." Andrei was a good man. Too bad, she wasn't good for him.

ANDREI WILLED HIS PULSE to slow to a normal rate. He waited at the edge of the hallway where he could watch both the restaurant floor as well as the bathroom Jocelyne had entered, vowing to never let the pretty redhead out of his sight again. When she'd vanished from the restaurant, his world spiraled out of control. He'd been back on the night of his sister's disappearance when the entire town had turned out to search for the two missing high-school girls.

He'd run out the back door into the thick fog and called out her name, holding his breath, pain tightening his chest, waiting for her to answer. Her lack of immediate response hadn't helped. He'd lost at least a year off his life in those few minutes he'd lost track of her.

Now, back in the restaurant with Jocelyne safe and accounted for, he had decisions to make. Did he continue to use her as his cover, or would that place her in too much danger? If he didn't continue the charade, he wouldn't have an excuse to stick to her like glue and make sure she stayed safe from the strangler. He couldn't stand back and let her go about town by herself no matter how much she insisted she could. A killer still lurked in the shadows of Raven's Cliff.

Mayor Wells had made it back to his seat next to Rick Simpson. Grant Bridges had disappeared. He must have left in the short time Andrei had been out of the restaurant. The mayor's assistant bent close to the mayor, his body tense, and his words too low to hear.

What difficulty was the mayor into now? Hadn't he been in enough trouble already, he should be keeping his nose clean? Wasn't it bad enough his own daughter, Camille, had disappeared and was as yet unaccounted for? When she'd fallen from the cliff at her own wedding, her body had never been found.

Andrei had been there when she'd fallen over the edge. The wind came up suddenly and surprised them all, especially Camille Wells. Had her fiancé, Grant Bridges, had anything to do with her "falling" over the cliff? Had he helped her along? No one could say for sure, but it didn't appear as though he'd had anything to do with her demise. Was he the Seaside Strangler operating in full view of the city of Raven's Cliff, getting away with the murder of innocent young women?

That burning fear and frustration that had gripped Andrei since they'd discovered the location of the henbane plant roiled in his gut. The thought that a killer could be living under the same roof as Jocelyne had him so tense, he couldn't sleep at night. The move into the inn couldn't happen soon enough. Tomorrow seemed like forever. He wondered if he could convince Jocelyne to let him sleep in her room for just tonight.

About the time she walked out of the bathroom, Mayor Wells and Rick Simpson rose from their chairs and headed for the front exit.

Jocelyne's gaze followed them.

Mayor Wells strode through without looking back. Rick Simpson, however, shot a glance over his shoulder, his gaze narrowing at Jocelyne, his expression inscrutable.

"Good," she said as Andrei seated her at their table. "I'm glad they left. Now we can eat in peace." She stared down at the plate of chicken *cordon bleu* with a side of asparagus and sighed. "What a shame."

"What's a shame?" Andrei sat beside her and lifted a fork to poke at the rib eye steak on his plate. "Looks good to me."

She smiled, her lips barely lifting upward. "This is the first time I've eaten here and I don't even feel like eating."

Andrei set his fork and knife down. "We need to talk."

"Haven't we talked enough for a lifetime?"

"No. I want to move into Cliffside Inn tonight."

"That's too short of notice for my mother to get you in. If I'm not mistaken, the rooms are booked for tonight. We may have an opening tomorrow night."

"Since we're supposed to be an item—" he crossed his arms over his chest and gave her a hard stare "—I can stay with you."

"You can what?" Her voice had risen and other guests in the restaurant stared at them. Jocelyne's gaze darted around and came back to him. She leaned forward. "You will not stay with me."

"After what happened tonight, do you feel comfortable being alone, even in your own room?"

"Yes." Her lips pressed together in a thin line, but a shiver wracked her body, belying her response.

"Yeah." Andrei lifted his fork. "I'll sleep on the chair or floor. You can have the bed."

Chapter Nine

Thank goodness for small favors and inclement weather. Hazel Baker was able to put Andrei in a guest room that night. A customer had called to cancel because of the incredibly dense fog. Sleeping in Jocelyne's room had not been a necessity and he managed to get a decent night's sleep on the overstuffed goose down mattress.

The thought of sleeping in the same room as Jocelyne… well, there wouldn't have been any sleeping. Close proximity with the woman had him on edge all the time, his body automatically reacting to the sway of her hips, the swell of her breasts and the sexy curve of her pregnant belly.

She'd made it more than clear that she didn't like the idea of him sleeping in the same room and argued all the way back to the inn. When her mother informed her a room was available, she'd let out a heavy sigh.

That sigh had been a bit unnerving, deflating Andrei's ego. What didn't she like about him? Had he imagined her response to the kisses he pressed to her fingertips in the restaurant? He could swear he'd seen the flare of passion in her eyes.

He'd obviously been wrong, or she was holding back for some other reason. Today, besides going over the interviews Mitch Chapman had conducted with the men who frequented the inn, Andrei promised himself he'd get to the bottom of Jocelyne's hot and cold attitude toward him. If they had something developing, he'd just as soon get it out in the open. If there wasn't, then he'd get on with the investigation and get out of her life.

The second option left him feeling flat and empty. He liked her fiery spirit and independence, and the way her red hair caught the candlelight and glowed with its own brilliance. Walking away from her now would be difficult when his protective instincts urged him to stay close. Those instincts went beyond Jocelyne to include the innocent baby she carried.

Andrei rose early, jumped in the shower and dressed in the same clothing he'd worn the night before. Without a razor, his face had a dark shadow of stubble. Couldn't be helped. He'd stop by his apartment for clean clothes and a shave on his way to the police station. First, he had to see Jocelyne.

Downstairs in the kitchen rich aromas of coffee, biscuits and bacon greeted the start of the day. Jocelyne glanced up at him over a large mixing bowl filled with creamy pancake mix, a soft smile lifting the corners of her natural, coral-colored lips.

Her smile warmed the morning chill from his skin. "I'm headed out. I'll be back later today. I'll start helping your mother with whatever she needs done around here late this afternoon, or tomorrow if I don't get back soon enough."

"I'll tell her."

Leah pushed through the swinging door. "Jocelyne, do you know where your mother keeps the extra napkin rings?" She stopped when her gaze encountered Andrei. "I'm sorry. I didn't mean to interrupt."

"You're not. I was on my way out." Andrei took the opportunity to play his role, slipping his arm around Jocelyne's waist.

When she looked up, her mouth opened, a retort ready to spring out.

Andrei didn't give her the chance to voice her objection. He bent and kissed her full on the lips, letting his mouth linger, the citrusy taste of orange juice tempting him to delve deeper.

The wooden spoon dropped from Jocelyne's hand and her arms stole up his chest, bunching his shirt in her grip.

"Uh…I'll be back when you two are done."

Jocelyne immediately stepped back, her cheeks flaming. "No, no. I'll show you where those napkin rings are."

He'd caught her off guard and answered one of his questions. No. She wasn't immune to him and she'd definitely returned his kiss. A chuckle rose up in his throat and he felt more optimistic about everything than he had in weeks.

Leah ducked back through the swinging door, with Jocelyne following. Before the red-haired beauty closed the door behind her, Andrei called out.

"Don't go anywhere until I get back."

Jocelyne stopped cold in her tracks and let the door close between her and Leah before she turned to face him, her cheeks still red, and her eyes burning bright. "What do you mean 'don't go anywhere'? I have a life to live. Not only do I help my mother with her business, I have one of my own. Surely you don't expect me to wait around for you to escort me all over town? I'm a big girl, I don't need you to take care of me. I won't let you." Then she turned and dove for the door.

Not before he grabbed her hand and tugged her back. "Promise me you'll stay inside until I get back." He brushed his lips across hers. "Please."

At her surprised look, he pressed his point, taking her mouth in a long, sensuous kiss. When he broke away, he whispered, "Promise me."

Her eyelids drooped over slumberous green eyes and she said in a breathless voice, "Okay." Then she shook her head, a hard glint replacing the sleepy look, her well-kissed mouth firming into a straight line. "But don't kiss me again." She pushed through the door, letting it swing violently back, almost hitting him in the face.

Andrei chuckled. The woman had sass and perhaps more control than he did. He rubbed a hand over his prickly jaw. Speaking of control, where had his gone? One touch, one taste and he'd lost himself in her. Not a good place to be when you were working a murder case. Especially when one of the murders was your little sister's. His light mood darkened.

Andrei exited the inn, determined to put Jocelyne out of his thoughts for long enough to make progress on the case. Although the fog was still thick, the daylight made it a little easier to move around. He set his car headlight beams on low and headed for the police station, parking at the rear of the building.

Mitch Chapman stood by his desk, thumbing through a file. "I thought you were fired." The burly cop with the light-red hair and ice-blue eyes looked up at him.

"I am." Pasting on a thin-lipped glare for show, Andrei stomped past Mitch. "I came to collect my things."

"I gotta get this to the captain then I'll help." He slapped shut the file and ducked into the captain's office.

Andrei nodded to several of the men in the office, striving for the sober expression of one who's been sacked. They'd all find out soon enough that his firing had been a cover. For now, they'd be kept in the dark, thinking he'd overstepped his bounds. Not a good thing for a new guy on the job.

Mitch returned, carrying an empty computer paper box. "Sorry about your disagreement with the captain. We'll miss you around here."

"Yeah. Same here."

The officer led the way through the maze of desks, stopping at Andrei's, setting the box on its cluttered surface. "Did you decide what you'll do next?"

"I'm moving into the Cliffside Inn to help Hazel Baker out

with odd jobs." He shrugged. "I'll look for full-time employment in a couple weeks. Maybe I'll go back to New York."

"Not enough excitement for you here in Raven's Cliff?"

"More than I ever wanted. More than my family deserved." Hell, if he had it all to do over, he'd have stayed in New York, fighting bad guys he could see. Then his sister, Sofia, would still be alive. He loaded the personal items from his desk top and rifled through the drawers making a show of packing his stuff. When he'd finished he held out his hand. "Been nice working with you, Mitch."

Mitch nodded. "Take it easy, man."

The other men in the room called out goodbyes as Andrei strode past, their faces drawn.

Andrei hated the pretense. Had he been on the force longer, these men would be more like brothers than mere acquaintances. He hoped that after this case was solved, he could come back and make more of a difference in his and their lives.

As he passed the captain's glassed-in office, he nodded at the man who'd been his mentor.

"Lagios!" The captain's voice carried through the glass.

With a scowl pasted on his face, Andrei entered the office. "Yeah, what?"

"Two things. The first…" Captain Swanson rifled in his desk, making a show of pulling a file out. He dropped the folder into the box Andrei had filled with his personal belongings. "This is your file. You might need it the next place you go," his said, his words loud enough to be heard by anyone walking by his open door.

"Thanks, but I doubt I'll go back into law enforcement."

With a subtle wink, the captain nodded. "Second, they found a hair in the bracelet Angela Wheeler was wearing the night she was murdered," he said in a whisper. "See what you can do to gather hairs from our suspects."

With his back to the door, Andrei spoke in a low, barely audible tone. "Why didn't you do that when you had them in for questioning?"

"Didn't have that piece of info until five minutes ago." Captain Swanson nodded toward the door. "You better go. Call me with an update when you get a chance."

Andrei stared down at the file Mitch had brought to the captain moments before. The manila folder was marked SS Suspect Interviews. A thrill of anticipation rose in Andrei's chest. He had the interview transcripts. He glanced up at the other man, maintaining a disgruntled look he'd practiced before he'd arrived at the office. "Good luck finding the Seaside Strangler, Captain. You're gonna need it." Then he headed for his apartment, a shower and a thorough reading of the transcripts. Hopefully, he'd find something that pointed to a killer.

"WHERE'S HAZEL?" LEAH STRODE into the kitchen following afternoon tea, her arms loaded with a tray of dirty dishes.

"In the basement. What can I help you with?" Jocelyne dried her hands on a dish towel.

"My son's school just called and he's not feeling well. Do you think she'd mind if I left a little early today? I don't have anyone else to take care of him."

"Go." Jocelyne took the tray from Leah's hands and set it on the counter. "I'll take care of the dishes and cleanup. Your son needs you."

"If you think it'll be all right…" Leah already had her apron untied and was reaching for her purse beneath the counter. "I hate to think of him sitting in the nurse's office for too long."

"Go. We can handle the rest."

"Thank you. I owe you one." Leah left through the front entrance. She walked to the inn five days a week in the dark of early morning and walked home by three, stopping to collect her two young sons from school.

Jocelyne gathered the remaining dishes and cutlery from the dining room and set her hip against the swinging door and backed into the kitchen. When she turned with her laden tray she screamed and nearly dropped the tray, dishes and all.

A dark figure stood framed in the back doorway, his face all but invisible beneath a hooded cape.

"I'm sorry, I didn't mean to startle you," he said in a deep quiet voice, turning his face away from her and backing through the doorway.

"It's okay. Don't leave." Jocelyne set the tray on the counter and pressed a hand to her chest. Her heart beat in a wild erratic rhythm. "Do you always sneak up on people?"

"No, ma'am." His hood swayed side to side.

"I certainly hope not." The baby kicked and rolled, mirroring her distress. She pressed a hand to her belly, the snug turtleneck sweater forming to the swell.

When the man's blue gaze followed the movement of her hand, a chill slithered down Jocelyne's back and her arm dropped to her side. This man in the hooded cape was just too mysterious, too weird and he was giving her the creeps.

"Mr. Jackson? Is that you?" Hazel Baker's voice called out from the bottom of the basement stairs. "Come on down here. I have your balm."

"Pardon me." He pulled the hood closer and crossed to the staircase, dropping down into the darkness like a thief descending into hell.

Jocelyne dragged in a deep breath and let it out. She hadn't seen this man since she'd been home, but her mother apparently knew who he was and did business with him. Was he a regular? Should she add him to her list of potential suspects?

Jocelyne busied herself scraping leftovers into the trash and loading the industrial dishwasher, keeping her ears open for anything that might sound suspicious. Several times she hovered near the basement door, dreaming up reasons to go after the man. The quiet hum of voices reassured her that her mother was indeed all right and the man wasn't attacking her.

When he finally came up, he kept his head down and his face averted from her scrutiny. He'd left before she got a decent look at him. Her first and last impression was one of shadows.

Her mother came up a minute later, carrying a small white paper bag.

"Mom, who was that man?"

She stared around as if looking for someone. "Do you mean Mr. Jackson?"

"If he's the one who was wearing the cloak and hood, yes. Mr. Jackson who? I don't recall a Mr. Jackson in all of Raven's Cliff. Is he new?"

"Well, yes, actually, he hasn't been here all that long. Maybe a couple months or so. Nice enough, from what I can tell."

"How often does he come to the inn?"

"Once a week for balm."

"Once a week?" Definitely a man to watch. "Does he always come to the basement for this balm?"

"Why, yes, of course. He doesn't like to be seen in public so he comes down to conduct his business in the basement. Sometimes he orders food delivered to the little cottage he lives in. You know the one. That old seaside cottage on the edge of town."

Jocelyne's eyes widened. "The one that's practically falling down?"

"Yes, dear." She set the bag on the counter next to a casserole dish, gathered her trench coat and a hat from the coat rack and put them on, hiding a huge yawn behind her hand. "I'll be out for a little while." Hazel lifted the bag and the casserole dish and turned toward the front hall, her steps slow, her face drawn, the circles under her eyes more pronounced than usual.

Jocelyne laid a hand on her arm. "Are you feeling all right, Mom? You don't look well."

"I suppose I'm a little tired." She yawned again. "But I promised Lucy I'd get this casserole and her migraine remedy to her today."

"Lucy Tucker at the Tidal Treasures shop?"

"That's her." Hazel smiled at her daughter. "It's okay, I'll be right back."

"Don't be silly, Mom. I'll take it. You go lie down." Jocelyne took the casserole dish and bag from her mother's hands and set them on the counter. "You've been on your feet since four this morning. You need a break."

"If you're sure."

"Not a problem." Jocelyne grabbed her jacket from the coat rack in the corner and slid her arms into it. "I need some fresh air, anyway."

"If the shop's closed, take it upstairs. She lives in the apartment over the store." Already her mother was shedding her coat. "Don't take too long, dear. That fog's still hanging around and it'll be dark quicker because of it. You sure you're up to it? You're the one who's pregnant, not me."

"Pregnant, not weak. Don't worry, Mom. I'll be right back." She hadn't forgotten her promise to Andrei, but her mother really did look tired and she wouldn't feel right about letting her go after she'd slaved all day at the inn. Compared to the little bit that Jocelyne did, her mother was a one-woman dynamo. Her body had to give in sometime.

The fog from the previous night had hung over the coastline for most of the day, a few rays of sunshine managing to poke through once or twice, but not enough to warm the air. With the wind nonexistent and the tide out, an eerie calm filled the hovering gloom.

Three blocks from Cliffside Inn, Tidal Treasures sat on Main Street two buildings down from Driftwood Lane. When Jocelyne arrived in front of the glass windows painted with colorful shells, sand dollars and hermit crabs the lights were off inside. She tried the door, but it was locked. Lucy had to be upstairs already, having given up early on business.

Jocelyne peered down the alley, the fog and late afternoon shadows making the narrow space between the buildings a murky cavern.

A chill shook her body. With her hands full of casserole and remedy, she couldn't wrap her coat around her tighter so she endured the damp creeping beneath her lapels. With a deep breath of salty humid air, she plunged down the alley. After only a few steps, her eyesight adjusted to the darkness. At the end of the alley, she turned left and almost tripped over a set of wooden stairs leading up to a landing and a doorway. No welcoming light shone over the landing or the staircase.

"She'd better be home," Jocelyne said out loud as she climbed the stairs to the landing and knocked on the door with the hand holding the paper bag.

After several seconds and no answer, she knocked louder.

She'd just turned to leave when a thump and a muttered curse alerted her to movement inside the apartment.

"Lucy?" she called out, her pulse ratcheting up several notches. Was the woman in trouble or hurt? Jocelyne waited, barely resisting the urge to test the doorknob. As she reached out to do just that, sounds of footsteps reached her through the wooden panels.

"I'm coming." The door swung open and Lucy stood there in flannel pajamas with tiny seagulls covering every square inch of fabric. Her short, curly, strawberry-blond hair stuck out at odd angles, red lines streaking the whites of her baby-blue eyes. She pressed a hand to her head and moaned. "Oh, Jocelyne, is that what I think it is?" She reached out her hands like a man begging for water in a desert.

When Jocelyne held out the casserole, the other woman grabbed the bag instead and turned back toward the tiny kitchenette in the corner. "Thank God." She grabbed a glass out of the cabinet and filled it with water from the tap. "I've had a migraine all day. Didn't even make it downstairs to open the shop."

"I'm sorry to hear that."

"If it weren't for your mother's miracle cures, I'd be a complete basket case." She pulled a folded wafer of wax paper from the bag Jocelyne's mother had sent and poured its powdery contents into the water. After a quick stir with her finger, she upended the glass, swallowing every last drop of the water and powder. "I'm sorry, I'm not much company. You're welcome to come in." She waved to the side with one hand while reaching into a drawer for a cloth with the other. With her eyes closed tightly, she held the cloth under the kitchen faucet and groped for the cold water handle, twisting it until the water ran over the cloth.

"I really can't stay. I came to deliver the migraine remedy and this casserole Mom sent."

"What a dear. I totally forgot I'd ordered that. I don't even feel like eating. Oh, that reminds me, I need to cancel my date with Alex. He'll be disappointed, but I just can't."

"Do you want me to leave him a message?"

"Would you?" She twisted the excess moisture out of the cloth and pressed it over her eyes. "The thought of lifting a phone to my head is as appealing as driving bamboo shoots up my fingernails."

Jocelyne winced and strode across the floor to the refrigerator. "I'll just leave this in the fridge. When you're feeling better you can stick it in the oven and heat it up."

"Thank you. You're a dream." She staggered back toward the single bedroom. "I'm going back to bed to smother myself beneath a pillow. Would you lock the door on your way out?"

"Do you get these migraines often?" Jocelyne asked the retreating figure.

"Every once in a while. Must be when I drink alcohol. I

went out with Alex last night and had a couple glasses of wine. I woke up this morning with a migraine that wouldn't quit." She pulled the cloth from her eyes and squinted at Jocelyne over her shoulder. "I'm giving up wine. I can't live like this."

"Is there anything I can do for you?"

"No, just leave me here to die. Thanks for bringing the powder. I'm not even sure what's in it, but it helps…" she sighed "…after a while…"

Jocelyne twisted the lock on the door and tested the handle on the other side. "Hope you feel better soon. Bye, Lucy." She closed the door, the lock clicking in place before she remembered to turn the outside light on.

Clouds and fog had choked out what little light remained from the late afternoon sun, cloaking the town in murky shadows. The absence of streetlights at the back of the building, coupled with the low ceiling of fog hanging close to the earth made it impossible for Jocelyne to see a darned thing. She felt her way down the steps, gripping the handrail like her life depended on it.

When she reached the bottom, she let out the breath she'd been holding and put her hand out to find the wall. But her hand didn't find solid brick. It bumped into the slick fabric of a jacket and, beneath it, a solid wall of muscle.

Jocelyne opened her mouth to scream, but a hand clamped over it, cutting off the sound and her air supply.

Chapter Ten

After spending the day reviewing documents, catching up on phone calls and documenting what had occurred thus far in the investigation, Andrei was more than tired of being cooped up.

The interviews were inconclusive. Three out of four of the suspects didn't have an alibi for the night of Angela Wheeler's disappearance. The only man who did was Alex Gibson. He'd claimed he was with his girlfriend, Lucy Tucker.

A quick call to the owner of Tidal Treasures confirmed Alex's alibi. Not only did Lucy Tucker have a date with Alex that evening, he'd stayed the night in her apartment, taking care of her through a migraine headache. The entire night. That narrowed the list of suspects down to three.

Rick Simpson claimed he'd been jogging earlier that evening and then spent the night watching television. By himself. No witnesses. He did, however, have a history with Angela, stating he'd asked her out a couple of times, but she'd refused. Officer Mitch Chapman had made a note that Rick didn't look too pleased about being turned down. But that didn't make Rick a killer.

Mayor Wells had been out to dinner with his wife, dropped her off and went for a drive until close to midnight. He claimed he'd visited a pub in a neighboring town.

Andrei lifted the phone and dialed the man who'd conducted Wells' interview.

"Captain Swanson."

"It's Lagios."

"About time you called. What did you think about the interviews? Disappointing, huh?"

"Yeah." Andrei tapped the mayor's paperwork. "Did you send anyone over to the pub the mayor said he'd been at the night of Angela's disappearance?"

"Went there myself."

"And?"

"Nothing." The captain sighed. "None of the pub's waitstaff recalled seeing Mayor Wells there that night."

"Think someone is lying?"

"My bet would be the mayor is lying through his teeth. Especially after what happened to him last night at the Seafarer's Bounty. The man has some serious issues and some not so nice friends after his butt."

Andrei had already come to that conclusion. "He bears watching."

"Trent's already on it. Vance is tagged with keeping up with the assistant, Rick Simpson."

Andrei chuckled. "With Trent, Mitch and Vance around, the Chapman boys are a one-family police force in Raven's Cliff."

"Damned glad to have them, especially with you off the roster." The captain paused. "What have you learned at the inn?"

"Nothing more than what you know already. Practically anyone can get into that basement and steal henbane leaves. Jocelyne asked her mother to start locking up when she's not down there."

"Good."

"Other than Alex's alibi and Grant's weak story, we don't have much to go on. We need solid evidence."

Captain Swanson snorted. "Then we follow them around, snoop through their lives and hope something surfaces before another woman dies. Keep me informed, Lagios."

"Will do," he said and hung up.

Tired and frustrated, Andrei rose from his chair at his tiny dining table and stretched. Gray light filtered in through the vinyl blinds. The sun had never come out today and dark was already settling over the small fishing town.

If he were honest with himself, he'd delayed going back to the inn. He'd been determined to find something in the interviews. A clue he could sink his teeth and this investigation into. He didn't want to go back to Jocelyne empty-handed. Or was it that he was avoiding her altogether? Forcing himself to stay away during the daytime. The less contact he had with her, the better off she was. Or the better off *he* was.

Whichever the case, he'd had enough. He'd almost talked himself out of staying at Cliffside Inn that night, convinced that if he did, he might not be able to keep his distance from the red-haired, green-eyed witch who'd more than captured his attention.

Now that they had a concrete piece of evidence—the hair found by the ME—he needed to get into the mayor's office and collect a strand of the mayor's hair. While he was at it, he could get one from Wells' assistant. Tomorrow he'd stop by the courthouse first and then the DA's office to gather a specimen from Grant Bridges. No need telling them why. If he could pick up one off their desk chairs, the ME could rule out suspects pretty quickly with a quick look beneath the lens of a microscope.

In the meantime, he had to go back to the inn in case someone else stole into the greenhouse for more of the henbane plant.

He packed a duffel bag of clothing and descended the stairs that led to his apartment, flipping his cell phone open. Cliffside Inn was on speed dial and he hit the button, holding it down until the connection went through.

"Cliffside Inn, Hazel speaking."

"Mrs. Baker, Andrei Lagios. Is Jocelyne close to the phone?" He thought he'd pick her up and take her out for a walk along the beach to get her outside after being housebound all day.

"She's not back yet from making a delivery for me."

"Delivery?"

"Yes. She went to Lucy Tucker's with a casserole and some migraine remedy I made up for the girl. She should be back any minute. Want me to tell her you called?"

"No. I'll catch up with her." He flipped the phone closed and stuffed it into his pocket, his mind racing through the streets to Lucy's apartment even before he made it to his door. Two blocks over and one up. He'd get there faster on foot by cutting through yards and alleys. Andrei took off at a dead run, refusing to let anything interrupt or divert him from getting to Jocelyne as fast as possible.

Darkness had already settled over the community and, though not as thick as the night before, fog hung over the buildings, muting the streetlights and giving the streets a gothic, dangerous feel.

Andrei's elbows pumped, his lungs sucked in and processed massive amounts of air as he ran through an alley, leaped over a low hedge and dashed across two streets. No sounds stirred the still air except his heavy breathing and the way his shoes slapped against the pavement. When he reached Main Street, he swung left. A block away, a shadow detached from the sturdy pole of a public streetlight. It stood unwavering as though frozen in time. Who was it?

The shadow backed up several steps and turned as if to run.

"Jocelyne?" Andrei called out.

The figure stopped, completed an about-face, but didn't answer him for a long moment.

"It's me, Andrei." He strode toward the figure, more sure with each passing step, it was Jocelyne.

"Andrei!" With a strangled cry, she ran toward him, her coat flapping open, sobs echoing against the brick storefronts. Hitting him full-on, she plastered herself to his chest, her arms wrapping around his middle, holding him so tightly, he could barely breathe.

He stroked her back, liking the feel of her body pressed to his like a second skin. "Jocelyne, sweetheart, what happened?" After a minute, he set her far enough away from him to look down into her face. A streetlight revealed the trail of tears streaked down her cheeks, strands of hair stuck to her skin.

Andrei gripped her arms, his breath coming in gasps from his race through the streets. "What happened?" he repeated, smoothing the hair out of her face.

"Take me home," she said, her voice little more than a whisper.

"Are you hurt?"

"No. I'm okay. Just take me home." She leaned her forehead against his chest.

Gathering her to him, he held her without moving. "Can you walk?" he questioned softly.

"Yes." She pushed back, her arm curling protectively around her belly.

Andrei's heart skipped a beat. "The baby? Jocelyne, is the baby okay?" He stared down at the swell of her abdomen and his hand came up to touch her there.

Tears fell more freely down her face. "He threatened my baby. My God, he threatened my baby." Then she was in his arms, sobs shaking her body.

"Who, Jocelyne? Who threatened your baby?"

"I don't know," she wailed. "It was so foggy, I couldn't see his face, but his voice." Her frame trembled in his arms. "It was one of the men from last night. The one with the smooth voice."

"One of the men who pounded on the mayor?"

"Yes." Her arms circled around his waist again and she laid

her face against his chest. "He held a knife to my belly and told me if I didn't stop snooping, he'd kill my baby."

"No one is going to kill your baby, Jocelyne." He bent, scooping her up in his arms. "No one is going to get near enough to do anything to you or your baby." His arms tightened around her as he held her. He carried her the two blocks back to the inn.

"You don't have to carry me," she protested.

"We've been through this argument before." He kissed her nose and marched on. "Humor me, will ya?"

The rest of the way to the inn, Jocelyne curled against him, her hand resting on his shirt, her face pressed to his neck. Warm breath and the scent of some subtle flower assailed his senses. When he reached the inn, though his arms were straining, he didn't want to let her go.

"You have to put me down. I don't want to upset my mother."

He hesitated at the front door.

"Please, Andrei, put me down."

His name on her lips melted his resolve and he let her feet drop slowly to the ground.

"I don't want to tell her anything about what happened last night or tonight. My mother has enough to worry about without me adding to it."

"But, Jocelyne, she needs to know you might be in danger."

"No."

"At the least, I need to inform the captain."

"No." One hand rested on her stomach, the other clutched his arm. "Leave it. My baby deserves a chance. I won't risk my life or his anymore."

"I never should have involved you in this case." Andrei drew away. "This was all a big mistake."

"Andrei, it's not. Finding the killer is the most important thing right now. I'm just going to stay out of snooping around the mayor like a good little pregnant woman. Now, I think I'll go up to my room, shower, change and go to bed."

"I'm going with you."

She rested her hand against his chest. "I can do this myself. Just run interference if my mother makes an appearance. I don't know what I'd tell her if she asked me about my puffy eyes and red nose."

Andrei pressed a kiss to the end of her red nose. "You're beautiful."

An unladylike snort was her only response before she opened the door and made a dash for the stairs.

AFTER A WARM SHOWER, she dressed in her favorite fleece pajamas. With the elastic waistband pushed below her rapidly expanding belly, Jocelyne crawled into bed with a favorite book. For the next two hours she pretended to read, while jumping at every sound. When she couldn't take it anymore, she pulled the sheet up to her chin, purposely leaving the light on to chase away the shadows, both real and imagined.

Tonight had been a warning to her. She needed to stay out of this investigation or risk the life of her innocent, unborn child. Her hand pushed the hem of her shirt upward, exposing her baby bump, the smoothly rounded skin still pliable. She'd never wanted to place her child in danger, and she wouldn't if she could help it.

Having the tip of a wicked knife shoved against her where just a slip of the wrist could slice through the relatively thin wall of skin into the placenta and ultimately the tiny body, made her shudder just thinking about it.

When the man had left, and she'd stumbled out onto the street, dazed and in shock, she'd never been happier to see anyone than she'd been to see Andrei.

The warmth of his body against hers helped chase away the cold dread threatening to consume her. He'd been so patient, so caring.

The baby poked a foot against her bladder reminding her to go to the bathroom one more time before attempting sleep.

Jocelyne rolled out of bed and onto her feet, padding across the Persian carpet to the tiny bathroom.

What would she have done if Andrei hadn't shown up?

Hell, she'd have staggered her way back to the inn and locked the door to her room until the baby was born. But Andrei had held her and given her support, comfort and hope. For the third time since she'd known him, he'd carried her to where she'd needed to go. She needed to thank him and then tell him not to do it again. A man like that, she could get real used to having around.

And that wasn't an option.

Jocelyne completed her business, washed her hands and dragged her tired body back into the bedroom.

"You took long enough."

Jocelyne screamed and clapped a hand over her mouth when she realized the man seated on her chaise lounge was Andrei Lagios, not some psychotic mobster bent on harming her or her baby. But that didn't excuse him from scaring the living daylights out of her.

"What the heck are you doing in my room?" she demanded.

"What does it look like? I'm sleeping here." He tucked the fluffy white pillow he'd purloined from *her* bed beneath his head and leaned back, closing his eyes. "I suggest you do the same."

The sight of him wearing nothing but a pair of faded jeans, crisp dark hairs sprinkled liberally over his bare chest and a lock of hair dipping down over his forehead, nearly gave Jocelyne a coronary. Her nipples puckered against the inside of her flannel pajamas, rubbing against the fabric in a deliciously sensitive way. Low in her belly desire bloomed and unfurled, making her knees weak and her thoughts chaotic.

"Y-you can't sleep in here." Hell, she couldn't sleep here

if he was in the same room. Already her breathing had gone shallow and her pulse kicked into marathon mode. Didn't he have a clue how attractive he was? Didn't he understand how dangerous that attraction could be to her resolve…and his life?

He lay back, his face serene, and popped one eye open. "Are you going to stand there all night?"

"No." Who did he think he was? She was about to ask him that very question when she noticed the loose button on his blue jeans and the line of dark hairs leading downward beneath the thick waistband. Jocelyne's mouth parched as dry as the Mojave Desert in July, her tongue tied in a pretzel.

"Do you mind turning out the light?"

She opened her mouth to tell him what he could do with the light, but her voice and brain didn't engage.

While she scrambled for something to say, he opened his eyes again.

Jocelyne clamped her lips shut and stomped over to her bed, climbing in, pulling the blankets up to her chin. "Don't think I'm a pushover all the time."

A smile flickered across his lips. "I'd never think that of you. Jocelyne Baker a pushover?" He shook his head, crossing his arms over his broad muscular chest. "Not a chance."

Her eyes wide, her mouth dry, her brain fried, Jocelyne stared at the gorgeous man camped out on her lounge and despaired of ever falling to sleep.

"The light?"

She crossed her arms over her chest. "I'm not turning out the light."

"Turn it off, and I'll tell you the latest clue Gordon Fennell, the medical examiner, found."

"Did anyone ever tell you that you're a tease?"

He smiled. "Maybe a few girls in high school."

"A few?" She snorted and rolled to her side, pulling the brass chain on the old-fashioned, pink hobnail lamp on the night stand. The room plunged into darkness. "Okay, so spill."

Andrei chuckled, the sound like melted chocolate sliding down her throat. "They found a hair on a bracelet belonging to Angela Wheeler."

"So?"

He paused before answering in his low, resonant tone, "It wasn't hers."

Her pulse sped up for more reasons than this new clue. "You think it's the killer's?"

"That's the ME's guess. We need a hair from Simpson, Wells and Bridges to compare against. That might help narrow it down or rule them out altogether."

"What about Alex?"

"He was with his girlfriend on the nights of the murders. He has an alibi."

"A hair, huh?" Jocelyne tapped a finger to her chin.

"A hair."

"So, what's your plan to get them? Will you just ask the suspects to give you a hair?"

"I think we can get what we need without anyone knowing. Once we have a match, we can follow up with a legal request for a DNA test to be conducted."

A more substantial clue this time. What a relief. With a sigh, Jocelyne lay back against the sheets, her eyes wide, absorbing every bit of light they could in the complete darkness. Only she wasn't afraid of the gloom now. Not with Andrei in the same room, his voice a calming tone that soothed ragged nerves, at the same time it steamed the windows.

No, she wasn't afraid of the dark now. She was afraid of the growing feelings she had for Andrei. Did he feel it, too?

"Feel what?"

Her face heated, and she clamped a hand over her mouth.

After spending her young life hiding her feelings from a town that had scoffed at her mother, she'd have thought she'd be better at keeping her mouth shut and her feelings to herself. Jocelyne admitted her ten-year sabbatical from Raven's Cliff left her rusty at the art of deception.

"Feel what, Jocelyne?" he asked again.

"This thing between us." There, she'd said it. She'd exposed herself. Now she prayed she hadn't imagined his feelings for her. Had he really only played a good part as her boyfriend?

"Yes. I feel it." The low rumble of his voice warmed the cool night air filling the space between them with more promise than she'd felt in a long time.

The baby kicked. Inserting the silent reminder of why Jocelyne couldn't have a relationship with any man. "Don't, Andrei."

"Don't what?"

"Don't fall in love with me." Her voice came out as the barest of whispers she hoped he wouldn't hear.

"Why not?"

Damn the man for his super-cop hearing and damn herself for even bringing up this whole conversation. If she'd ignored it, it wouldn't happen. Bull! "I'm poison."

"Poison? I don't understand."

"The men who fall in love with me don't live. I'm like a black widow. It's just not safe for anyone to fall in love with me." Her voice caught in the back of her throat on a sob. More than anything, she wanted the chance to fall in love with Andrei, and wanted him to be free to fall in love with her. But she couldn't risk him.

The lounge creaked as he shifted and then the mattress sank beside her.

"What are you doing? Didn't you hear me? I'm cursed." She scooted to the opposite edge of the bed, her body on fire with the need to touch him, feel him, run her hands over his naked chest.

He slid beneath the blanket and reached for her, bringing her closer to all that skin stretched taut over hard muscles. "I heard you, but I'm not running. Just like I don't believe this town is cursed, I don't believe that you're cursed. It's all a bunch of hooey, as my mother would say."

Her defenses weakening, Jocelyne barely fought him as he dragged her closer into the curve of his body, fitting her against him and draping a large calloused hand over her hip. "Curses aren't real. People cause bad things to happen, not curses. Just like the Seaside Strangler. He's just a man—a crazy man—not a curse."

"Tell that to my mother," she said, her breath catching when her fingers connected with his bare chest.

The broad hand spanning her hip stroked her in ever increasing circles until his finger slipped beneath her top and found the curve of her waist.

Suddenly, her mother was the last person on Jocelyne's mind. But this was wrong. She couldn't let it happen. Much as Andrei laughed at the black widow theory, what else could it be?

He moved closer, his mouth brushing against the side of her neck. "Let me hold you for tonight. We can worry about everything else tomorrow."

How could she resist his sensual magnetism? Jocelyne melted into Andrei, letting him turn her so that her back was to him, spooning her in the sheets.

She didn't think she could go to sleep with her body on fire. The need to get naked with this man, to feel his hands all over her, to have him take her, love her as if tomorrow didn't matter overpowered her rational thoughts. How could anything that felt so right be a curse?

The hard ridge of his fly told the rest of the story. He

wanted her as badly as she wanted him, but he did no more than hold her.

Breathe in, breathe out. Jocelyne tried to concentrate, to hold back. After several meditation exercises and controlled breathing, exhaustion did the rest and Jocelyne closed her eyes. "Promise me, Andrei?"

"What, sweetheart?" A feathery kiss fanned her sensitive earlobe.

"Promise me you won't fall in love with me."

Andrei hooked his arm beneath her belly and stroked the skin stretching over her baby.

His gentle caress lulled her into the land between sleep and wakefulness. As she descended into slumber she thought she heard his response. But she wasn't sure, and she couldn't wake up enough to ask him to repeat it.

It went something like, "I can't promise you that."

Chapter Eleven

While Jocelyne slept, Andrei lay awake, his entire body a raging inferno of desire. All night he fought the urge to wake her and take her while her defenses were down. That she'd admitted her attraction only made it worse.

But she trusted him. Damn it, she trusted him, and he couldn't destroy that trust. Not with her silly notion that he was in danger if he fell in love with her. What had started as a need to gather evidence had transformed into a need to protect the young mother.

Instead of waking her to a beautiful act of lovemaking, he lay still, running through all that had taken place since they'd gotten the lead on the drug used on the murder victims. With the knowledge of who frequented the inn and the hair they'd found on the latest victim, they actually had something to go on. They could get a quick match under a microscope if one of the suspects' hairs closely compared to the one found on the victim. That would be enough to make an arrest until the DNA could be further tested for an exact match.

By the early, darkest hours of the morning, Andrei couldn't take it anymore. He couldn't lie still without exploring Jocelyne's curves. He slid out of the bed, careful not to wake her, and went back to his own room. There he poured through the interview documents one more time, learning nothing new, but satisfying that niggling doubt that he might have missed a clue.

What it came down to was that if he wanted answers, he had to take matters into his own hands and go after the evidence he needed. The sun hadn't yet made its appearance over the horizon, but the gray of predawn lightened the sky.

Lack of sleep gave Andrei's eyelids a sandpaper texture every time he blinked. Rather than go to sleep for only one more hour, he went for a jog around the town square, never straying too far from Cliffside Inn. He passed the courthouse where the DA worked and the mayor's office located in the police station next to the courthouse, formulating a plan to get those hairs he needed. When he returned to the inn, the sun had risen and with it Hazel Baker had begun her day, cooking breakfast for the boarders and patrons.

Up by five o'clock, Andrei fixed the leaky shower in one of the empty guest rooms, tightened the loose railing on the second-floor banister and replaced the batteries in the kitchen and dining-room smoke alarms, all before eight o'clock.

After a quick shower, he dressed in nice slacks, a crisp white shirt and a suit jacket, suitable for a job interview. First stop this morning would be the police station. The mayor's office was located on the second floor. Andrei would request an audience with the man under the pretext of applying for work. If all went well, he'd come out with a hair sample from Simpson and Wells. Then he'd swing by the courthouse where the assistant DA, Grant Bridges, had his office. Again, he'd go in job hunting.

When he left his room and descended to the ground floor, he saw Jocelyne at the base of the staircase. The morning sunlight lit her hair from behind, turning it to a dark copper, gilded with gold highlights. Her green-eyed gaze skimmed over his clothing. "Are you leaving?"

"I have some hair hunting to do this morning." He gave her a very slight wink and stopped beside her on ground level.

"Don't you want breakfast?"

"No. I want to get this over with. And the best time to catch people is when they first come into the office in the morning."

A local businessman entered through the front door. "Morning."

Before he responded, Andrei wrapped an arm around Jocelyne's waist. "Good morning."

The businessman passed through the open sitting area into the dining hall.

Andrei lifted a finger to her chin, tipping it upward. "Stay here, please. I don't want to worry about you, especially with a thug threatening you. As soon as I get back, I'll take you anywhere you want to go." He pressed his lips to hers in a feathery kiss, afraid if he delved deeper, he wouldn't come up.

Her breath caught on a sigh. "I'll be here when you get back."

"Promise?"

"I promise."

Ah hell, who was he kidding? He bent and took her lips, slanting across them, pushing his tongue past all barriers to twist around and stroke hers. She tasted cool and fresh like mint. When he finally pulled away, his mind was cloudy with need and completely unfocused. That's what this woman did to him. Knocked him off the rails.

Glassy-eyed, Jocelyne's lids drooped halfway down. Her hands rested against his chest, her calf curled around the back of his leg. When she realized her position, she quickly stepped back, her face turning a fiery shade of red. "I'll see you in a little while."

Andrei left before he succumbed to her full kissable lips once more. He had work to do, evidence to gather and a killer to catch. He certainly didn't have time to think about the way

Jocelyne had melted against him, her warm body pressed to his, her breasts peaked beneath the gold sweater she wore.

He pushed past her and exited the inn, striding across the town square toward the police station, his first stop. Tucked in his back trouser pocket were the paper sandwich bag purloined from the inn's kitchen and a pair of tweezers from his shaving kit—the tools he'd use to collect what he needed.

The police station was located at the opposite end of the town square as Cliffside Inn. Fortunately the courthouse stood next door. He'd have his evidence by noon, if not sooner. And maybe a few answers concerning the attack on Jocelyne. His stomach roiled every time he thought of the man threatening to stab a knife into her belly. Anyone sick enough to even threaten such an act wasn't human.

JOCELYNE WATCHED FROM A WINDOW until Andrei disappeared down Main Street, her lips still tingling from his kiss.

She wanted so much to give in to her feelings for this man and see where they led, but she couldn't. His life depended on her keeping her head and staying away from him. He couldn't fall in love with her. She wouldn't let it happen.

With that thought in mind, she strode into the kitchen and dove into helping her mother with breakfast preparations and cleanup. Anything to get her mind off the man who made her knees melt like butter on a hot plate.

As she lifted a wooden spoon to stir batter for pancakes her mind cleared of the fog his kiss had created.

Andrei said he was going after hairs from the three suspects on the list she'd made to compare with the one found on Angela Wheeler's bracelet.

Damn.

Jocelyne smacked her palm to her forehead. She hadn't told Andrei about the mysterious Mr. Jackson who'd stopped by Cliffside Inn the night before. He didn't know that Ingram

Jackson stopped by on occasion, descending into the basement for some of Hazel Baker's skin balm.

Part of her wanted to rush out right then to tell Andrei, but that could blow his cover of job hunting.

Jocelyne stuck the wooden spoon into the batter and stirred, thinking up ideas of how they could get a hair from a man who'd managed to remain a recluse in the small community.

The flash of a purple, gold and orange skirt flitted by, and her mother grabbed an oven mitt from a drawer. Then she whipped open one of the double ovens to rescue a tray of fluffy golden biscuits. "Flip the pancakes before they burn, Jocelyne."

She blinked, bringing herself back to the kitchen and the smell of rich brown pancakes frying on the skillet. She set the batter spoon aside and lifted a spatula, deftly flipping the round pancakes over to brown on the other side. "Mom, how often did you say Mr. Jackson comes in for one of your remedies?"

"Once a week. Which reminds me, he ordered a serving of my clam chowder for his evening meal. I need to remember that."

Perfect. "Mom, I'll take it over this afternoon. No need for you to go."

"It's not a bother. I don't want you getting all worn out working in the inn. You have your own business to run."

"I can do that during the day when the morning rush is over. That's the beauty of my work. I can set my own hours."

"That'll be great when my grandbaby arrives." Her mother rounded the counter and gathered her daughter into her arms. "Have I told you lately how glad I am you've come home?"

Jocelyne chuckled. "In between trying to get me to leave? Yes."

"I still worry about you, but I'm glad you're here." Her gaze captured Jocelyne's, her mother's green eyes a mirror image of her own. "I missed you so much."

A lump stuck in Jocelyne's throat and moisture gathered in the corners of her eyes. "I missed you, too, Mom." For so long, she'd avoided this town and her mother, resenting everything her mother stood for and the cruel taunts her schoolmates had flung her way.

Now that she had a child of her own on the way, she couldn't begin to imagine the pain of a mother whose child has rejected her.

She gathered her mother even closer and hugged her hard. "I'm sorry I stayed away so long."

"It's okay." Her mother held her at arm's length, a smile tilting her still-lovely lips. "You're more like me than you ever thought. You had to find yourself. I was fortunate to have your father to help me find myself when I was lost. And this town."

Jocelyne shook her head. "This town has given you nothing but grief."

"They can't help it, Jocelyne. It's natural for people to be afraid of what they don't understand."

Is that why she was so afraid of her attraction to Andrei Lagios? She'd never felt so out of control as she did with him.

Her mother kissed her cheek, her eyes glistening. "You're burning the pancakes, dear."

"I'D LIKE TO SPEAK WITH Mayor Wells." Andrei smiled at the mayor's secretary, using the Lagios charm to its full advantage on the single woman. Lydia Fleming was the name carved into the smooth black nameplate propped on her desk.

Her face flushed and her eyelids fluttered. "Mayor Wells will be here momentarily. Do you have an appointment?"

Andrei perched on the corner of her desk. "Not actually. I was hoping you could help me with that, Ms. Fleming."

"Lydia. Call me Lydia."

While Lydia's attention focused on the computer screen at

the inside corner of her desk, Andrei straightened and walked behind her to peer into the open door of the mayor's office. "So this is the mayor's office?"

"Yes, but he doesn't like people to go in while he's not here."

He ignored her comment and strode in, headed for the window behind the mayor's massive mahogany desk. "Wow, look at that view."

Lydia followed him in. "Really, Mr. Lagios, you shouldn't be in here. The mayor will be angry."

"I just can't get over the view from here. He's got a choice office here on the square. You can see the water from here." And Cliffside Inn. His chest constricted with need. The need to see Jocelyne. An overwhelming urge to protect the woman was taking over his life. Andrei wondered what she was doing now. Would she stay put at the inn like she'd promised?

"Really, Mr. Lagios, you shouldn't be in here."

Andrei glanced back at the secretary.

Poor Lydia, wringing her hands, she shot fleeting looks over her shoulder to the doorway.

"Andrei," he said with his most engaging smile. "Call me Andrei."

"Andrei," she responded, her voice soft and hesitant. "I can get you right in with the mayor if he's okay with it. He doesn't have anything scheduled."

"That's great." Andrei turned and placed his hands on the back of Mayor Wells' leather chair. "The mayor's a lucky man to have you, Lydia."

Her face turned a delicate shade of pink. "Thanks. If you'd like to wait out in my office…"

"I've always wondered what it would be like to be the mayor." If he was going to find a hair, the chair was the best bet. Now, how to dig around in the cushion without the nervous secretary having a coronary. He swiveled the chair around and sat in it, sliding his hand into the crease between the back and seat cushions. "Making decisions that affect the town, having all that responsibility."

"The mayor will be here any moment."

Before he turned back to the secretary, he managed to gather enough lint and dust from that dark recess the cleaning staff couldn't see. He stuffed the lint glob in his trousers pocket and stood, rounding the desk.

"What the hell's going on here?" Mayor Wells strode through the doorway, carrying a polished leather briefcase and sporting a frown that didn't fit with the image he portrayed while campaigning. The bruise over his cheekbone had faded to purple with a tinge of green, on the way to healing.

"Mayor Wells." Andrei plastered a smile on his face and held out his hand. "Glad you could see me on such short notice."

"What do you mean? I don't recall having an appointment with you." He turned to Lydia. "Do I have an appointment with this man?"

"Sir, you do now. You didn't have anything on your schedule for the next hour, so I thought it would be all right." She edged toward the doorway leading back to the safety of her desk.

Caught between Andrei and his secretary, the mayor slammed his case onto the top of his desk. "Fine. I'll see him."

Lydia cast a brief smile at Andrei and shut the door as she left.

"What do you want, Lagios?"

He wanted answers, but first he had to feel him out. "Two things." Andrei stood with his feet wide, his arms crossed over his chest. "First, I wanted to speak to you about employment opportunities with the city."

"What happened with your job at the police department?"

"The captain and I had a difference of opinion."

"Well, you've come to the wrong place. See the HR lady in the courthouse. I don't keep up with city job openings." The mayor opened his briefcase and pulled out several files, tossing them onto the desk.

"What I had in mind is more personal." Andrei's expression remained casual, but there was nothing casual about what he'd say next. "I thought you might be in the market for a bodyguard."

The mayor's glance shot up, his eyes narrowing. "What gives you that idea?"

Andrei nodded at the bruise on the mayor's cheek.

"I'm not looking for a bodyguard."

"Well, if you decide that you need one, you can find me at the Cliffside Inn. I'm living there for the next couple weeks."

"I prefer that you and your girlfriend stay out of my business."

Andrei's muscles tensed. "Why's that? Are you still in some kind of trouble?"

"Not at all." The mayor stared at him long and hard. "I just don't want anyone getting hurt."

Andrei's hackles rose at the mayor's blunt words. "Is that a threat?"

"No, consider it a warning." The mayor walked to the door and opened it. "Now, if you don't mind, I have work to do."

Rage seared through Andrei's veins like liquid fire. He stalked up to the mayor and closed the door. "Tell your 'friends' to lay off Jocelyne Baker."

"Friends? What friends?"

"Your friends who did this." Andrei flicked a finger at the mayor's bruised cheek.

Mayor Wells flinched, his hand rising as if to deflect a blow. "Has Miss Baker been threatened?"

"Yes."

The mayor straightened, his mouth firming into a thin line. "I had nothing to do with what may or may not have happened to Miss Baker."

"Wrong answer." Andrei closed the gap between them,

standing toe-to-toe with the man. "Understand this…if any of your 'friends' threaten or hurt her or the baby she's carrying, like they did last night, I'll come looking for *you*."

The mayor's brows tipped upward. "Is that a threat, Mr. Lagios?"

His lips tightening, Andrei shook his head. "No, Mayor Wells. That's a promise."

Chapter Twelve

The noise-producing roar and steady motion of pushing a vacuum cleaner only helped pass the first hour. After two hours spent scrubbing the inn, Jocelyne's back hurt and the baby bounced against her ribs, protesting the noise. Pushing a roaring machine around the rugs on several floors of the inn helped drown out her thoughts to a certain extent. She'd taken over the vacuuming because sounds were making her jump. Then because the vacuum was so loud, people had to tap her on the shoulder to get her attention. She jumped every time.

And speaking of time…could it creep any slower? She watched the windows for Andrei's return, anxious to get on with the task of hair collection.

On more than one occasion, she considered entering Grant Bridges' room to collect a hair from his comb or brush. Each time, she thought about when he'd caught her outside Alex's room, and a chill jolted down her spine. If she had a lookout, she'd be all right. But who could she tell what she was up to besides Andrei? She came back to the same answer. No one.

She had to wait for Andrei. For someone who liked taking charge of her own life, waiting wasn't easy.

Having cleaned everything she could clean and packaged orders to be shipped the following day, she'd run out of things to do and worn herself to a frazzle wondering when Andrei would come back. Jocelyne settled into an overstuffed sofa in front of the roaring fire in the great room on the first floor. The sofa faced the front entrance, all the better to watch for Andrei. She didn't much care if she looked anxious to see him. She was.

At exactly three o'clock that afternoon, Andrei walked in through the front entrance.

Jocelyne had just turned to stare into the fire when the hinges gave a tiny squeak despite the oil she'd applied earlier that day. Her head whipped around.

Andrei walked in wearing the suit, tie and long trench coat he'd had on earlier that morning. His dark hair, dark eyes and rugged good looks made him appear as though he'd just stepped off the cover of a magazine.

With her stomach turning somersaults, Jocelyne remained seated until she had her breathing in control to avoid fainting from hyperventilation. "You're back." Of all the stupidly obvious things she could have said…

He crossed the huge room, his shoes tapping against the wooden flooring. "I had a few stops to make. Some took longer than others."

Jocelyne couldn't help taking a quick glance around. Still early in the afternoon, most of the residents hadn't arrived back at the inn for dinner. She sighed. "All this cloak-and-dagger stuff has me jumpy. Did you get what you were looking for?"

His sexy lips twisted. "Some. Not all. I sent off what I did get to the crime lab."

"Anyone I can help you with?"

"No. I don't want you involved any more than you already are. It's too dangerous."

"At least tell me who you didn't get."

"Bridges."

Jocelyne smiled. "I can help you with that."

"Did you hear me?" He gripped her arms, his hands warm despite having just come in from outside.

"I can get the keys to his room. He usually doesn't come in until after four." His hands heated her in all the wrong places, and she pulled back, afraid of his nearness and the rush of her pulse. "At least let me get the keys. We could say you're fixing a toilet leak or something. I'll keep watch."

Andrei shook his head, a smile tilting the corners of his lips upward. "Are you always this stubborn?"

She crossed her arms over the top of her belly and gave him a narrow-eyed glare. "Yes."

"That's what I thought." He scrubbed a hand through his thick dark hair. "Okay. Although it's against my better judgment."

When she smiled, he waved his hands at her. "Hurry it up, will you? Bridges will be here before you know it. I'm going to change into jeans. Meet you on the second floor."

Jocelyne scooted through the dining area and peeked into the kitchen. Already busy with dinner preparations, her mother stood in front of the stove, adding ingredients to a stockpot. From the smell of it, clam chowder was on the menu for the evening's dinner. Jocelyne's stomach rumbled. Clam chowder was one of her favorites. She hadn't had anything as good as her mother's since she'd left home.

Clam chowder meant an automatic delivery to one of the other people who visited the basement. Ingram Jackson.

Jocelyne grinned. She'd let Andrei in on that little gem of information after they took care of Bridges.

She let the swinging door close quietly without disturbing her mother and hurried down the hallway to Hazel Baker's suite and the hidden keys.

When she returned to the empty living area, she didn't slow down, taking the steps up to the second floor two at a time.

At the top of the landing, she paused to breathe and then

turned left while glancing back to the floor below. That's when she ran into a solid wall of muscles.

"Careful." Andrei held her away. "Are you okay?" He glanced down at her, staring into her eyes for a brief moment before his gaze dropped to her belly. "Both of you okay?"

His words had a way of making her feel desirable and cared for. All that wrapped in one smooth-as-melted-chocolate voice settled her ragged nerves and set them on fire in one breath. "I'm—we're fine." Her hand rose protectively to her baby bump. She shoved the other hand toward him. "Here are the keys. Second door on the right. I'll watch out from here."

Andrei closed his fingers around the keys, engulfing her hand in one of his. "You're beautiful."

Heat climbed up her neck into her face until she thought her hair might catch fire. "You, too," she said, and meant it. She'd never met a man so perfect. From his midnight-black hair, ebony eyes, lips made for kissing and shoulders broad enough to care for two—make that three.

Whoa. Wait a minute. She couldn't go there and pulled her hand free. "Beat it."

Andrei dropped a kiss on her lips, executed an about-face and entered Grant's room, closing the door behind him.

Skip tingly and go straight for full-throttle sizzling. The man knew how to make her want more. Jocelyne shook her hair back as if she could shake the man out of her system. *Fat chance.* The door downstairs opened, causing her heart to miss two beats, effectively drawing her attention back to what she was supposed to be doing.

Leah, one hand on the door, looked over her shoulder. "See ya tomorrow, Jocelyne."

Jocelyne waved and made her lips form into a smile. Would she ever get used to this spy business? She hoped it wouldn't become a habit. As it was, everyone was a suspect in her mind and within every shadow lurked a bad guy waiting to kill innocent women and babies.

ANDREI MOVED THROUGH THE ROOM with quiet precision, searching for any evidence linking Grant Bridges to the murdered women. The man kept his room as neat and clean as an army barracks. Not a stray document, knickknack or hair out of place in the bedroom. The antique dresser remained free of all clutter, the smooth cherrywood stood unscathed from time and abuse, smoothly polished to a glossy finish.

Andrei opened the drawers, one by one, revealing neatly folded shirts, socks and even underwear. In the top right drawer, he found a framed picture of Grant and the mayor's daughter, Camille. Their engagement picture showed two un-smiling people. How odd. They should have been happy about announcing their engagement, shouldn't they?

As far as Andrei was concerned, Camille's fall from the cliff made Grant a prime suspect in her disappearance, although no one could prove Bridges had pushed her. The RCPD had chased that horse to a dead end.

As clean as the bedroom, the bathroom was testament to what an anal-retentive man could do when he had an inclination to keep everything tidy in his life. Not Andrei. Invariably, some item of clothing would find its way to the floor and he'd leave it there for days before collecting it for the laundry.

The housekeeper in the inn must be taking care of the man to the extent every item of clothing had a place and was in it. Andrei opened the closet to neatly organized suits, casual wear and shoes lined up along the floor. No hairbrush or comb, no clues to the murder mystery eating at Andrei's con-science. A glance at his watch made him hurry toward the open door to the small bathroom. Inside, the countertop was barren of all toiletries except a toothbrush stand with a single blue toothbrush sticking out of one of the holes.

Andrei opened the medicine cabinet. Inside, on the bottom ledge lay a plain black comb. Bingo.

Upon closer inspection, Andrei discovered the comb was as neat and clean as the room. No hairs.

He pushed the shower curtain aside scanned the bathtub for loose hairs, finally locating one.

The outer door opened with an almost imperceptible click. "Time to wrap it up, Bridges just drove up."

Using a pair of tweezers from his pocket, Andrei lifted several broken hairs from the tub and slid them into an evidence bag. Then tucking the tweezers and bag into his pocket, he hurried out, closing the door behind him.

Jocelyne stood at the balcony railing, her hands clasped together, her gaze darting to the floor below.

The front door opened and Grant Bridges walked in, his gaze rising to the two people on the landing in front of his room.

With no time to think, Andrei spun Jocelyne into his arms and pressed a kiss to her lips. Her mouth opened on a gasp, allowing him to deepen the contact.

What started as an attempt to cover his snooping changed into blood-thrumming, heart-pounding need. His hands slid into her silky red hair, continuing down her back to press her hips to his. The warmth of her body, the sensuous press of her breasts to his chest, igniting his cells into an inferno.

Instead of backing off, as usual, Jocelyne leaned into him, her tongue flicking out to connect with his, her hands climbing up his chest to intertwine behind his neck. Her breathing grew shallow and her legs parted around one of his thighs.

"Eh-hem," a voice said from the stairs.

Andrei broke the kiss, stepping back.

Grant climbed the stairs and stood on the landing, his lips twisted in a look of disgust.

"Excuse me." Jocelyne's pale cheeks bloomed with rosy color, her green eyes glassy, her lips swollen and thoroughly kissed. A hand rose to smooth her hair. "We'd better go check on that thing we were supposed to check on, shouldn't we?" She stared up at Andrei.

He almost laughed at how flustered she sounded. Instead he hooked her arm in his and squeezed by Grant. "Excuse us."

Bridges frowned as they passed him. "My secretary said you wanted to see me."

Andrei nodded to Jocelyne. "I'll meet you in the kitchen."

She nodded, her gaze darting back to Grant, but she left.

Once Jocelyne had made it halfway down the winding staircase, Andrei turned back to Grant. "I came by to inquire whether the DA's office had any openings."

The other man stared at him through narrowed eyes. "Not that I'm aware of. What did you have in mind?"

"Investigative work, bodyguard, security?"

"I thought you were with the Raven's Cliff PD?"

"I was. The captain and I weren't seeing eye to eye." Andrei shrugged. "We agreed to disagree and parted ways. I'm looking for work."

"Must have been a significant disagreement." Bridges was fishing.

Andrei wasn't biting. "It was personal."

Grant's scrutiny lasted for a moment. "I don't think we have any openings right now, but speak with my secretary. Now if you'll excuse me…" He turned toward his door, pulling his keys from his pocket.

Andrei's heart rate ratcheted upward. He'd forgotten to lock the door. Not much he could do but leave Grant to wonder. He descended the steps as casually as possible. When he reached the bottom, he dared a glance upward.

Bridges stood in his doorway, staring back down the stairs at Andrei, his lips pressed in a tight line, his brows drawn together.

Let him wonder. Andrei headed for the kitchen, almost bumping into Jocelyne when he pushed through the swinging door.

She grabbed his arm and hustled him into the pantry. The dry, not unpleasant scent of flour and spices wrapped around him, settling his nerves. No need to worry Jocelyne with the unlocked door. Perhaps Grant would think the maid left it open.

Jocelyne snapped the light on and closed the door behind her, shutting them into the small, tight closet. "Did you get it?"

He nodded. "That should be all our current suspects."

She shook her head. "We have one more we need to collect."

"What do you mean?"

"I forgot to tell you, but Mom has another visitor who comes down in the basement to get her remedies. One who only enters through the back door and doesn't like to be seen."

"Who?"

"Ingram Jackson."

"The recluse?"

"That's the one. I ran into him yesterday coming for some balm. Apparently he has some pretty wicked burn scars."

Andrei drew a hand down over his face. "That could present a problem if we can't get a sample from him."

Jocelyne's face lit in a smile. "I have a solution."

Her smile made him want to reach out and kiss her again, but he clenched his hands at his sides. "And your solution is?"

"Delivery." The pretty smile widened. "Seems Mr. Jackson has a hankering for Mom's clam chowder and always has some delivered to his house on his housekeeper's night off."

"And this is the housekeeper's night off?"

"Exactly."

He couldn't hold back any longer. The eager expression and spark in her green eyes had him mesmerized. Andrei's hands reached for Jocelyne's arms and he drew her to him.

Her bright eyes widened, her mouth forming a rounded O.

"Has anyone ever told you that you have very kissable lips?"

Her head moved from side to side. "No."

"Well, you do." To prove it, he lowered his mouth to hers, exploring her lips in a long, sliding kiss that left him as breathless as it left her.

She was the one to push away, her tongue darting out to skim over where his lips had been. "You shouldn't."

He didn't let her go, barring her from running out of the pantry, running away from him. "Jocelyne, I don't believe all that eyewash about black widows and curses. What I do believe in is what I'm feeling." He released his grip and let his fingers slide down her arms to capture her hands. "You can't deny it, either, can you?"

She didn't meet his eyes, but stared down at where their hands were clasped. "It won't work. Something bad will happen to you."

"I'll take that chance."

"You might be willing to take that chance—" her chin rose and she peered into his eyes, hers swimming with unshed tears "—but I'm not." She jerked her wrists free of his grip and darted for the door, flinging it open in her mad rush to escape.

Andrei smiled. He had her scared, and she'd only be scared if she cared about him.

"Oh, there you are, Jocelyne." Hazel Baker's eyes widened when she noticed Andrei behind her daughter. "Oh, Mr. Lagios. Are you lost?"

"No, ma'am. And I'm sorry I haven't been around to help out, like I promised."

"I understand. Now, if you'd like to start work today, I have a delivery that needs to be made to one of my customers." She smiled at Jocelyne. "I know you said you'd do it, but I don't feel comfortable sending you out there on your own."

Jocelyne didn't argue as Andrei would have expected, instead she nudged him with her elbow.

He rubbed his ribcage and grinned. "I'd be happy to deliver whatever it is you need delivered, Mrs. Baker. All I need is directions and the item."

"It's going to Mr. Jackson on the edge of town." Jocelyne's mother rubbed her hands together and turned toward the stockpot full of bubbling chowder. "Well, then. That gives me time for a little project I have cooking, and keeps Leah from having to make a mad dash before the dinner crowd descends."

Andrei executed a mock bow. "Anything to help."

"And I'll show Mr. Lagios where Jackson lives," Jocelyne added.

Shooting Jocelyne a glare behind her mother's back, Andrei said, "No need, Miss Baker. I can find my own way."

"I'll help by holding the thermos. We wouldn't want any of Mom's clam chowder to spill, now would we?" she said through gritted teeth and a fake smile.

"That would be nice, dear. And it'll get you out of the house. I know how much you love being out and about." Hazel tossed a smile over her shoulder at Andrei. "I'm so glad you're here. It's handy to have another man around."

"Mrs. Baker, there's no need for your daughter to go with me. The cool air can't be good for the baby." He tipped his head toward Jocelyne in challenge.

"Oh, please." Jocelyne crossed her arms over her chest, her eyes rolling. "I need to get out or I'll go stir-crazy. It's settled. I'm going with you."

Andrei frowned, but short of an argument, he was stuck with her.

"Good." Hazel Baker filled an industrial thermos with the steaming chowder, stacked it in a box and laid a Baggie full of crackers in beside it. "Now, hurry before it gets cold and before that storm blows in." She handed the box to Andrei.

"What storm?" Jocelyne asked.

"The one that's been threatening all day, dear."

"It's been foggy all day. Not a hint of wind."

"I know, dear." She patted Jocelyne's arm like a not-too-bright child. "Since there will be a storm tonight, don't take too long. Oh, and Mr. Jackson likes his meal set out for him on the table, with the correct cutlery, if you don't mind." Before Jocelyne could argue further, her mother descended the steps into the basement.

For a few moments, Andrei stared after Jocelyne's mother. "How does she know there's going to be a storm?"

"Maybe she has aching joints. I don't know."

Andrei stood in front of Jocelyne. "Storm or no storm, you're not coming. It could be dangerous."

"I'm going and, no, it won't be dangerous. We're just delivering soup. And while I'm setting it out, you can collect the hair you need."

Andrei stood for a few minutes wanting to argue, but realizing Jocelyne was probably right. "Okay, but no questioning the man. I don't want to corner a killer with you in the house. Promise?"

She held up two fingers. "Scout's honor."

Andrei snorted and headed for his car. "Like you were ever a scout."

"I could have been." She climbed into the car, buckled her seat belt and held out her hands to take the box of chowder and crackers, settling them in her lap.

"Yeah, and I'm the Easter Bunny." Andrei rounded the car and slid into the seat.

With a town the size of Raven's Cliff, it didn't take long before they pulled in front of the old cottage on the very edge of town where Ingram Jackson lived. A solitary man, no one in town knew much about him. A perfect candidate for a serial killer.

A bad feeling pinched Andrei's gut as he shifted into Park and stared out at the lonely cottage, the gloom of a cloudy day shrouding it in mystery. "Look, let me take care of this. I don't want you in there."

"It's already settled. I'm going to set the table while you find the hair. Remember?" She didn't give him time to argue, but stepped out of the car carrying the chowder, and marched to the doorway.

Andrei hurried to catch up to her, sliding in front of her to knock on the door.

"Come in!" A shout sounded from somewhere inside.

Andrei glared at Jocelyne and took the box from her. "Stay here." With the box in his hand, he had to wait for Jocelyne to open the door.

When she did, he stood in her way. "Please."

"I'm going to set the table as my mother directed. Nothing more. Relax." She pushed past him and entered.

Relax? They could be walking into a trap.

"Mr. Jackson? It's Jocelyne Baker from the Cliffside Inn with a delivery for you." She took the box from Andrei.

"Set it on the table in the dining room." Again, a deep voice called out through the walls.

Jocelyne passed a hat-and-coat stand near the doorway. A black hooded cape hung from the top hook. She jerked her head toward it as she hurried by.

Andrei stepped into the small entryway, fishing in his jacket pocket for his tweezers and evidence bag. A few brown hairs stood out against the deep black of the cape's fabric.

Before he could reach for the hair, a shadowy movement flashed in the corner of his eye. Andrei swung toward a half-open doorway to his left.

"Who is that with you, Miss Baker?" Jackson demanded from his hiding place.

Jocelyne shot a startled glance at Andrei across the dining

table in the room to his right. "It's just my boyfriend, Andrei Lagios. He promised to take me out after I dropped off this clam chowder."

The shadow shifted behind the door and disappeared.

Andrei couldn't tell if the man still watched him. "Do you want me to wait outside, babe?" he called out to Jocelyne, who was setting the thermos on the dining table.

"Mr. Jackson, do you want my boyfriend to wait outside?" she asked.

"That's not necessary, Miss Baker," Jackson called through the wood paneling of the door closest to Andrei.

"I'll be done in just a minute, honey," Jocelyne said.

Warmth stole through Andrei at her casual endearment. Warmth that had no business claiming him in his current situation. He had work to do and Jackson was sneaking around his house like some criminal preparing for attack.

"Mr. Jackson, where do you keep your flatware?" Jocelyne was a good distraction and, despite his arguments to the contrary, Andrei wouldn't be able to collect the needed evidence without her.

"You'll find what you need in the kitchen." The voice came from deeper inside the room, farther away from the entrance hall.

Edging closer to the cape, Andrei's fingers closed around the tweezers and he eased them from his pocket. "Don't forget we have reservations for five o'clock at the Seafarer's Bounty."

"I won't." Jocelyne emerged from the kitchen carrying cutlery and a bowl. "You're going to love this clam chowder, Mr. Jackson. My mother makes the best in all of Raven's Cliff."

While Jocelyne talked, Andrei reached out for the hair closest to him, all the time watching for movement in his peripheral vision. He snagged the hair, whipped out the little evidence bag and dropped it in. When he reached for the second one, a footstep made him jerk his hand back.

"Maybe it would be best if you waited outside, Mr. Lagios." Jackson's voice vibrated through the wooden door.

"I'm done here." Jocelyne stepped up beside Andrei and hooked his arm, a smile spread across her pretty face. "Ready?"

Andrei slipped an arm around her waist. "Yes, ma'am."

"Enjoy your meal, Mr. Jackson." Jocelyne tugged Andrei toward the door.

The ominous shadow lurking behind the doorway shifted. Andrei insinuated his body between the shadow and Jocelyne. If Jackson jumped out, he'd have to go through Andrei to get to her.

Once again, Andrei could kick himself. This whole spy thing was all wrong for a pregnant woman. He shouldn't have brought her. Now the best he could do was to get her out as quickly as possible.

Chapter Thirteen

Jocelyne glanced over her shoulder at the tiny cottage sitting at the edge of town with the looming backdrop of low, steel-gray clouds. Fog drifted in from the ocean, as if cloaking the house in the shadow of suspicion. A shiver rattled down her spine at the possibility of that house being the home of a serial killer. She could have been serving chowder to a man who killed young women for fun.

She turned in her seat and faced the strong and sturdy silhouette of Andrei Lagios and relaxed a little. He'd been with her the whole time, providing the strength of purpose and protection that made everything okay. "Did you get it?"

He nodded as he pulled out of the drive and onto the road headed back into Raven's Cliff. "I did."

"Whew!" Jocelyne collapsed against the back of her seat. "All that hiding behind doors gave me the heebie-jeebies. I thought he was going to jump you for a minute there. Do you think he saw you take the hair?"

"I'm not sure, but the important point is that I got it. If any of these hairs are a match, we'll have to go back and collect official evidence to make it legal."

"Right, but at least we would know where to concentrate our efforts."

Andrei jammed on the brakes and pulled to the side of the road.

Her heart hammering against her chest, Jocelyne gripped the armrest. "What the hell did you do that for?"

Turning in his seat, Andrei shot her a narrow glare. "Let's get something straight. I didn't like you being in that man's house." When she opened her mouth to protest, he raised his hand. "Let me finish. If Jackson is the killer, you were in danger. I don't like putting you or your baby in danger. So when I say 'we,' I mean the Raven's Cliff PD, not you and me. Got that?"

"But—"

He pressed a warm, calloused finger to her lips. "No buts." His finger slid across her lip, his gaze capturing hers in the lights from the dash.

Jocelyne's breath caught in her throat and she completely forgot her argument, so trapped by his look she melted into the deep black of his irises.

His fingers slipped to the back of her head and gently tugged her hair, tipping her head back.

He was going to kiss her. Tingling warmth filled her chilled body. The cold reality of her past tried to dampen the warmth. She couldn't let him destroy her defenses with a kiss. A kiss she wanted more than her next breath. "Please, don't kiss me, Andrei," she said in a ragged whisper.

"Then stop me." His head lowered until his lips hovered over hers. "You've got all the power."

"I should make you stop." For someone with all the power, why were all her senses spinning out of control? In spite of all her internal warning flares bursting, Jocelyne's hands slipped up his chest to circle around his neck. "But I can't." She pulled him closer and their lips met in a fiery kiss that stole her breath away.

A car flew by, the motion buffeting their vehicle, reminding her that she was sitting on the side of a road, kissing a man she'd sworn not to get involved with. A man she didn't want to die because of her. No matter how good it felt to kiss Andrei, how would she feel if he died because of her curse?

Jocelyne slid shaking hands between them and pushed against his chest. "We should get back. Mom needs help getting dinner out for the guests."

His fingers lingered on her arms until another vehicle honked, passing by them on its way into Raven's Cliff. Andrei shifted into Drive and the car surged forward. "I'll drop you at the inn. I want to get these samples to the station and processed as soon as possible."

Silence reigned over the remainder of the journey to Cliffside Inn. When Andrei pulled up in front of the old mansion, Jocelyne sat for a minute trying to think of the right thing to say and came up blank. Finally, she pushed the door open and jumped out.

"GOT SOME SAMPLES FOR YOU." Andrei dropped the evidence bags onto the captain's desk.

Captain Swanson rose and hurried to close the blinds over the glass window of his door. "Did anyone see you come in?"

"No. I snuck in past the desk while Riley was talking to Mitch. The office is pretty empty due to shift change."

Captain Swanson thumbed through the bags reading the names off. "Bridges, Simpson, Wells…" He paused when he got to Jackson. "What's this?"

"Jocelyne discovered another man who's been frequenting Hazel Baker's little basement garden." Andrei paced across the room and back. "What do you know about Ingram Jackson?"

"About as much as anyone." The captain shrugged. "Not much. I'll get Mitch to interview him for his whereabouts on the night Angela Wheeler disappeared. And I'll get these over to the ME so they can get a quick ID on these compared to the one found on our latest vic." The captain left his office, carrying the evidence bags.

Instead of leaving, Andrei continued pacing. Nervous energy surged through his system with no relief in sight.

Swanson returned. "I thought you'd be gone. Is there something else?"

"No." Andrei pushed a hand through his hair. "Yes."

"Find something? Another clue?"

"No. It's just the Baker woman."

"The witch?"

Andrei glared at the older man. "She's not a witch, and that's not the one I was talking about."

A smile spread across the captain's face. "Has Jocelyne Baker got you tied in knots?"

"No…yes!" He spun away from the captain and breathed in, letting it out in a deliberately slow, steadying exhalation. He turned back to his boss. "I don't like that she's involved in this investigation. It's too dangerous."

Captain Swanson spread his hands. "What do you suggest?"

"I don't know. By now the entire town thinks we're an item."

"Then break it off and make your breakup public."

Knowing how much Jocelyne hated being the center of attention, he couldn't do that. She'd been laughed at as the daughter of the town kook, he couldn't bring public humiliation down on her. "I can't do that."

"Is she tired of the arrangement? Does she want out of it?"

How many times had she pushed away from him? She really believed he was in mortal danger if he fell in love with her. A hint of a smile lifted his lips. She always thought of others over her own desires. "Maybe."

"Then let her break it off and make it public enough that word gets out quickly."

"I think it's too late." For more than one reason. "I think she's in too deep into this investigation. She's asked too many questions." And he was in too deep with Jocelyne. He didn't want to break it off, despite her warnings that he would only end up hurt or dead.

"Then what are you going to do?"

Andrei's fists tightened into hammers. "Find the damned killer."

JOCELYNE HEADED STRAIGHT FOR her room on the third floor to splash water on her heated face. She kept reminding herself she shouldn't have feelings for Andrei Lagios. He was a good man and didn't deserve the heartache or danger of being involved with her. If only she could keep that in mind when her body ignited in his presence.

After thoroughly drying her face, and changing into a black turtleneck and loose-fitting jersey pants that didn't pinch her expanding waistline, she descended the stairs in search of her mother.

Leah moved amongst the guests, laying out bowls of steaming chowder.

"Leah, what are you doing here?" Jocelyne asked.

"My husband got the afternoon off, so he took the boys fishing. I offered to come back and help out. I can use the extra hours."

"Have you seen my mother?"

"She's been down in the basement for the past hour. I had to stir the chowder several times to keep it from burning."

Jocelyne's heart skipped a few beats. What was her mother doing in the basement when customers filled the dining room?

She hurried toward the kitchen, a knot forming low in her belly. The baby rolled over, poking a tiny foot against her ribcage. "It's okay, sweetie." She rubbed her belly with one hand and shoved open the swinging door to the kitchen with the other.

Her mother emerged from the basement, carrying a bucket of dark nasty liquid and a basket loaded with candles and incense.

Warning bells exploded in Jocelyne's head. "Mom, where are you going?"

Her mother smiled. "I'm going to put an end to this curse, darling."

Jocelyne grappled with what she could say that would stop her mother, knowing once she got something in her head, there was no deterring the woman. "You can't. The dinner crowd's already here."

"Everything is ready and Leah is here to serve. Besides, this shouldn't take too long." Her mother headed for the back door.

"Mom, no." Jocelyne hurriedly ducked around her, blocking the exit. "Don't do it." She could already envision the townsfolk following behind her mother, ridiculing her and calling her names. She couldn't let her go.

But her mother had the same stubborn streak she'd instilled in her daughter, either through her actions or genetics. Her smile turned upside-down, a deep frown emphasizing the wrinkles in her forehead. "I have to do something to save this town. The curse is undermining the good nature of its people, eroding families and destroying livelihoods. We can't let it go on."

"Mom, please." Jocelyne laid a hand on her mother's arm. "Please don't do this."

"Dear, either help me or move out of my way. Someone has to do something."

When her mother moved forward, Jocelyne had no other choice but to step aside.

Before Jocelyne could gather her jacket and change into sturdier shoes, her mother was halfway down Main Street.

Oh, geez. Please don't let people make fun of her. Jocelyne ran out the door, a stitch in her side slowing her to a walk.

By the time she caught up to her mother, a small crowd had gathered around the woman. With her bucket of icky stuff on the ground beside her, she stooped, setting four candles out in a circle. A green one at the north end of the circle representing Earth, a red candle at the south end for fire, a yellow one at the east side for air and a blue one at the west end for water. Then one by one, she lit each, the still, foggy air cooperating, creating a halo glow around each flame.

Jocelyne recognized the ritual from the hundred times she'd witnessed her mother performing it in her bedroom. Memories flooded back like brackish water in a tidal lagoon. Jocelyne held her belly and suppressed a moan. Is this what her child had to look forward to? A grandmother who practiced witchcraft and townsfolk laughing at her and the rest of her outcast family?

Hazel lit a stick of sandalwood incense, the smoke spiraling upward, mixing with the low-hanging clouds of mist.

Unfortunately, the fog had thinned sufficiently that Hazel Baker could be seen through the haze from most of the storefronts along the street. Those who were just leaving their businesses at the end of the long workday wandered over to watch her weave her spell.

With her eyes closed, the well-intentioned witch clapped her hands three times.

The crowd grew silent but for a few twitters of giggles.

Then Hazel Baker began her chant in a low steady voice, starting out barely audible, her volume growing until her words reflected off the clouds.

"Lady of the Night, Mistress of the Day
Please hear me call, I am your daughter
Mystic Woman of the Moon, watch as I lay

This Circle of Divine Power.
Great Father, Lover, Son and Hunter
Hear my call
Eternal Man, Gentle Man, watch over us
In this Circle of Divine Power."

"What's the old witch doing, now?" Rick Simpson eased up to the edge of the crowd, muttering to a well-dressed woman wearing a soft-gray suit skirt and matching overcoat.

If Jocelyne wasn't mistaken the woman was the mayor's wife, Beatrice Wells. She wrinkled her well-bred nose. "Looks like she's casting a spell or something."

"Probably cursing every one of us." Wasn't that the town librarian, Helen Fisher?

Jocelyne bit down on her tongue to keep from saying something she might regret or from drawing attention to herself.

"Oh, be quiet, Helen," Dorothy Chapman said. "It's not like you have room to talk."

From what Jocelyne had heard, Helen's brother, Theodore, had been experimenting with the fish population in the area and almost had everyone poisoned with a growth nutrient he'd secretly added, infecting the fish and the people who ate it.

The librarian huffed, her nose tipping in the air. "I wasn't my brother's keeper."

Dorothy leaned over the person's shoulder in front of her and called out, "Hazel, what are you doing?"

Jocelyne's mother looked up and blinked several times, her eyes widening when she looked around at the crowd. "This town has been cursed far too long."

"Who's to say you didn't put the curse on us to start with?" Helen yelled back at her.

"Me?" Hazel's brows rose. "Of course I didn't curse this

town. Nicholas Sterling did that. I'm trying to cure it." She closed her eyes again and lifted her head, her arms rising.

> "'Tis the time of the Goddess
> The time of the full moon
> The time of ancient power
> Make our dreams
> Live our lives
> Be with us as one
> 'Tis the stirring of all ages
> Where the Goddess comes into being
> She lives within us
> She is the power
> Together, we are one
> Blessed be."

Jocelyne's mother lifted a ladle full of the dark liquid and tossed it between each of the candles, chanting as she went.

> "I invoke Thy mercy
> Oh, please, come to us, Mighty Mother
> Bringer of all that is beautiful and peaceful.
> I invoke Thee by water, earth and fire.
> I invoke Thee by love and grace
> And call upon Thee
> To bring peace unto this place
> Cleanse it of all that is evil
> And rid us of the poison
> That tears us apart from within.
> Hear with my ears,
> Bless with my lips,
> Touch with my hands,
> Speak with my tongue,
> Fulfill this request

And bring peace to our home.
Blessed be."

Hazel Baker raised her face and arms to the sky, her eyes closed. A breeze stirred the mist, lifting the hem of her skirt in a light flowing motion. Her neat French twist unraveled, her long graying red hair tumbling down her back, buffeted by a puff of air.

A shiver rippled down Jocelyne's spine and she hugged her arms to chase away the chill beneath her skin.

Rick Simpson snorted. "Sounds like a bunch of voodoo-hoodoo, if you ask me. Are we going to let her get away with it? Hasn't this town had enough troubles without a nutcase stirring up more?"

"She's going to make it worse." Helen Fisher's eyes widened, her face paling to a sickening, waxy-white. "She's going to make the curse stronger!"

"I don't know about curses or whatnot, but I don't like the smell of that stuff. It can't be good," a fisherman commented. "She shouldn't be pouring it on the ground. It's probably some violation of EPA or something. Someone stop her."

Hazel ignored the whispers, continuing around the circle, dipping into the liquid and tossing it to the north, east, south and west. Fog swirled around her, giving each candle's flame a glowing, halo effect. All the while Hazel chanted in a low steady tone, her words no longer audible or understandable, a language only she could define.

The whispering voices surged.

"Stop her!" Helen Fisher yelled. "Stop her before we're all murdered in our sleep by the Seaside Strangler!"

"No. She's only trying to help." Alex Gibson stepped forward, standing between Hazel and the crowd. "She's only trying to help this town."

"She's poisoned your mind as well," Helen accused.

The crowd swelled, shoving Helen against Alex.

The man's face reddened and he tried to set her away from him.

When he grabbed her wrists, she screamed, "Let go of me!"

People poured out of the buildings, the crowd growing in size and intensity. The gray of a shrouded sunset descended like a cloak on the town, the streetlights flickering like glowing orbs suspended in space.

Hazel's eyes opened and she cried out, "Don't cross into the circle. Please, don't break the circle."

A dozen people trampled over the imaginary line, kicking over candles, dousing the flames, bumping the bucket of potion. The liquid inside sloshed over the edge into the grass, before righting itself.

Tears welled in the older woman's eyes, spilling down her cheeks. "No! Please, you don't know what you're doing. I'm trying to cure the town, not hurt it. You're going to make it worse."

Caught between people, Jocelyne couldn't move, the sounds of her mother's distress squeezing the air from her own lungs. "Move." She elbowed a fisherman in the side and pushed her way past a woman shaking her fist in the air. "Let me through."

"Why, so you can curse us as well?" Rick Simpson's voice sounded in her ear.

Uncaring of her own feelings, Jocelyne shoved Rick Simpson to the side and pushed through. "Leave her alone. She wants to help you all." When she finally made it to the broken circle, her mother had fallen to her knees, her face buried in her hands, her shoulders shaking with silent sobs.

"Get back, damn you. Damn you all. Get back." Jocelyne shoved at the crowd, making room for her mother. "Damn it, leave my mother alone!"

Helen gasped and pointed at Jocelyne. "See? She's cursing us!"

The crowd grew angrier and more violent. A rock flew through the air, glancing off Jocelyne's temple.

Pain shot through her head, and she staggered, warm blood trickling down the side of her face.

"We want her gone. She's the problem, not the cure," Helen shouted. "Go away, Hazel Baker, and take your daughter with you before she brings her devil's spawn into our community."

A collective gasp rose from the people gathered around and the crowd stood still.

"That's right, she's pregnant and there's no father." Helen turned toward the townsfolk. "The baby is devil's spawn, do you hear me? Devil's spawn."

Chapter Fourteen

After poring through the case files and coming up with nothing, Andrei emerged from the police station onto Main Street. A hefty wind had dispersed the fog, leaving the streets clear for the encroaching darkness of rain-laden clouds. On the opposite side of the town square, angry shouts filled the air and a mass of townsfolk converged on three figures.

Above the yelling and screaming, a female voice rose, "Cut her some slack! All she ever wanted was to be a part of the town, to make it whole and happy again."

Andrei recognized the voice instantly and every protective instinct in his body sprang to attack mode. He charged across the grassy square and into the surging throng. "Move. Step aside."

He pushed and shoved, making little headway through the crowd, catching glimpses of Jocelyne, her mother and Alex Gibson.

The older Baker woman crouched on the ground, gathering candles and a burned-out incense stick, tears falling from her eyes.

Jocelyne stood firm, her fingers curled into tight fists, her head thrown back with a streak of deep-red blood streaming down her cheek from a wound at her left temple.

Andrei's gut clenched.

A woman raised her arm, a rock in her hand.

"Drop the rock!" Andrei told her, his voice hard and cold enough to freeze the woman's arm in midswing.

The woman darted a glance his way and the rock rolled from her fingertips, dropping noiselessly to the ground.

Pushing on through the crowd, Andrei felt as if he was swimming in a sea of molasses. Every face turned toward Hazel and her daughter, all their anger and attention focused on the defenseless women.

"My mother loves this place—why, I'll never know—and all you've ever been to her is ugly, name-calling ingrates." Jocelyne stood in front of her mother, protecting her from flying stones and sticks. "She'd never hurt any one of you. She only came out here to help. To help people who have only ever shown her hatred and disrespect. Well, to hell with you all! If you want to get at my mother, you'll have to go through me first." She raised her fists and braced her feet, ready to take on anyone who wanted a fight.

"Don't let her scare you. She's just a woman. A pregnant one, at that. I say run them out of town." Helen shook her fist in the air. "Run them out of town before she gives birth to that devil's spawn she's carrying."

"She's not carrying devil's spawn. Don't talk to her that way." Alex Gibson's face burned bright red, his eyes wide and glassy. "Leave her alone."

Another fisherman shoved him to the side. When Alex grabbed his arm, the man threw a punch, knocking Alex into several other people. They pushed him to the side and rushed forward.

At the same time Andrei broke through the crowd and beat the fisherman to the redhead. "Touch her and I'll break every bone in your body." He stood in front of Jocelyne, his fists held before him, his tone deadly.

"Don't, Andrei." Jocelyne laid a hand on his arm, her voice

quiet but firm. "I don't want you involved. You'll only get hurt, like Mr. Gibson. Step aside."

"I won't let this town bully you," he said his voice rising above the shouts. "You all are tense and angry. Don't mistake what you're feeling for justice. These women have done nothing to hurt you."

"Nothing?" Helen screeched. "They've cursed this town with their witches' tricks. Four women have died due to their meddling curses."

"It's not us." Hazel shook her head, her face haggard and blotchy from crying. "It was young Nicholas Sterling who incurred the curse when he didn't light the beacon. If only he'd lit the beacon, none of those women would be dead." Wind whipped her hair into her face, giving her the appearance of a bedraggled old hag.

Alex Gibson climbed to his feet and reached out to help Hazel stand. "She's right. This town was cursed the night the lighthouse burned. The sea is claiming its due, just as it did the night Captain Raven's family died all those years ago."

"Right, and I'm Captain Nemo." Rick Simpson turned to face the crowd in his best facing-the-jury pose. "You're just trying to scare these fine people with your potions and hexes."

Andrei stepped up to tower over Simpson. "There's no such thing as a curse. Hazel and Jocelyne Baker are no different than any one of you."

"How can you say that?" Helen demanded. "They're self-proclaimed witches."

"And you're a self-proclaimed Christian." Andrei crossed his arms over his chest. "They want the same thing you want…peace for Raven's Cliff. A happy place to raise a family. The killing to stop." He didn't shout, but the wind tossed his words in their faces and the crowd stood still and silent.

The first drops of rain galvanized them into action.

The mayor's wife unfurled an umbrella. "Well, I have a dinner party to go to. Richard, are you coming?"

With one last look at Andrei and the Baker women, Simpson cupped Beatrice Wells' elbow and steered her through the crowd toward the sidewalk. "We'll have to hurry if we don't want to be drenched."

Andrei stood his ground, daring anyone to throw another stone or vicious comment at Jocelyne and her mother. One by one, the crowd dispersed, driven away by the steadily darkening sky and the increase in cold, heavy raindrops.

Jocelyne, the bucket in one hand and her mother's elbow in the other, stepped up beside him. "I didn't need your help, but thanks." She led her mother back toward Cliffside Inn, hurrying before the clouds opened up.

"They were only trying to help." Alex Gibson rubbed his midsection, a pained expression pinching his brows together. Then he, too, headed for the inn.

When he finally stood alone in the middle of town square, the rain pelted him like stinging, icy needles. He'd witnessed a town turning on some of its own people—defenseless women. Their behavior was a testament to the tension building among them over the unsolved murders.

No one wanted to find the murderer more than Andrei did, but a witch hunt wasn't the way to do it. For all he knew at this point, one of the people in the crowd that had turned on the Baker women could have been the killer, or he and Jocelyne had just served the Seaside Strangler a very nice meal of clam chowder.

Andrei's fists clenched, the cold water dripping down over his uncovered head and inside the collar of his jacket. If Ingram Jackson was the killer, he hoped like hell he choked on his last meal.

Meanwhile, he needed to get back to Jocelyne. The terror of being cornered by a rabid mob had to be enough to drive her to the edge.

"I NEED TO GO OUT AND FINISH what I started." Hazel grabbed the bucket of potion Jocelyne had set on the kitchen floor and headed for the back door. "It's worse than I thought. The town has gone crazy with the curse. The only way to cure it is to go to the lighthouse."

"No, Mom." Jocelyne removed the bucket from her mother's fingers. "You're not going out. In fact, go pack your bags, we're leaving this town and all its self-righteous citizens."

"Leaving?" She stared at Jocelyne as if she'd lost her mind. "I can't leave when they need me more than ever." She reached again for the bucket. "My potion will help. Really. If you'd just let me finish. I need to take it to the lighthouse and do the same ritual there. That's where it all began."

"You're not going out in this storm. It's wicked out there. I won't let you do it."

Her mother shook her head, her eyes sad and worried. "Someone has to do something, dear. Before it's too late."

"Fine, then I'll do it. After that, we're leaving." She grabbed the bucket by the handle. "I remember why I hated this town for so long. Because it hates us."

"No, Jocelyne. Don't hate it." Her mother's tears welled again in her red-rimmed eyes. "Raven's Cliff was a beautiful place before your father's death and before the curse. Your father loved it."

"Well, Raven's Cliff doesn't love us." Jocelyne's eyes burned and her head ached. "Let me have the bucket. I'll take it to the lighthouse and perform the ritual."

"But you're pregnant and injured. You don't need to be out in your condition." Her mother grabbed a clean washcloth from a drawer, ran water over it and dabbed at Jocelyne's face. "Let me go, it's getting dark and you don't need to be out in that storm."

"Right now that storm would be a warmer welcome than what the so-called good people of Raven's Cliff gave us. I could use a little fresh air, even if it's cold, dark and miserably wet." Jocelyne pushed her mother's busy hand aside and collected what remained of the bucket of slop and the basket containing the candles and a wrinkled copy of the spell her mother had dumped on the counter. "You stay here and get dinner out for your customers. They're waiting. I'll be back later. Don't wait up."

To avoid Andrei, Jocelyne left through the back door, crossing to her compact car where she laid the basket on the back seat and carefully set the bucket of potion on the front floorboard. Once out of town, she could dump the stuff in a ditch and be done with potions and witchcraft.

As she pulled out of town, she knew she couldn't destroy the potion and lie to her mother about it. Hazel Baker, resident witch, wanted to cure this town of the evil. Her heart was in the right place, but Raven's Cliff didn't want her cure. Right now, Jocelyne was ready to try anything. Her own heart ached from the look of terror and confusion on her mother's face when the people of Raven's Cliff had mobbed her.

For the first time in her life, Jocelyne wasn't humiliated by her mother's actions. No, she was more ashamed by the reactions of the people of Raven's Cliff. That they could turn on a woman who was trying to help them in the only way she knew how, was a horrible blow to her mother. So Hazel Baker was a little kooky. The last time Jocelyne checked, being kooky wasn't a crime, nor was it dangerous.

With one hand on the steering wheel, she wound along the crooked road to the lighthouse, patting the smoothly rounded bump where her baby grew inside her womb. *My poor baby. They called you devil's spawn.* Putting aside her concerns over her mother's well-being, how could she bring up a child in a place where people dared call her baby devil's spawn?

She didn't know, but she'd be damned if she let them drive her mother out of the only home she'd known since she'd come to Raven's Cliff as a young bride. She had just as much of a right to live in the town as any of the others. Probably more of a right. She cared enough to do something to lift the curse. What were the others doing? Nothing!

Except the undercover cop, Andrei Lagios. A man who wasn't far from Jocelyne's thoughts. He'd stepped in to side with Jocelyne and her mother, facing down a mob of angry people for them, even when others considered her crazy. Yet another reason to fall in love with the man.

And another reason for her to stay away from him. He deserved a woman who could love him for a long, long time. He deserved a long life, not one cut short by the black widow of Raven's Cliff.

Despair welled up inside her chest and she choked back a sob. Jocelyne couldn't tell if the driving rain on the windshield or her own tears blinded her, making her miss the turn to Beacon Manor and the lighthouse. As the side road raced by her peripheral vision, she slammed on the brakes, her rear tires sliding sideways.

Her seat belt tightened around her shoulders and hips, jerking her back against the seat. For a terrifying moment, she thought she'd smash into a fence. Instead the car slid into the ditch, its right side buried to the axles in run-off and mud.

The bucket of potion teetered, but righted itself.

"Damn!" She shifted into Reverse and gently tapped the accelerator. The car rocked and then the wheels spun, gaining no purchase in the roadside sludge. Jocelyne smacked her palm against the steering wheel, glad she hadn't injured her child, but mad for having allowed herself to become so distracted by thoughts of Andrei Lagios, she'd forgotten her goal.

The charred lighthouse stood like a ghostly aberration in darkening sky and icy rain. She'd come this far, she might as well perform the ritual, disperse the potion and then look for a way home. A chill snaked down her spine as she reached into the glove compartment for a flashlight and butane lighter. Then she gathered the basket of candles. With her hands grasping the handle of the bucket and balancing the basket, she pushed her door open and stepped out into the rain.

The wind and rain slapped against her face as if warning her away from the ill-fated lighthouse. Jocelyne could think of better ways to spend a stormy evening than trudging through rain and mud to cast a curse-lifting spell. But she'd made a promise to her mother and really…how much worse could the night get?

ANDREI ENTERED THROUGH the front door of the inn, going immediately to the kitchen in search of Jocelyne. He found her mother, setting out tureens of clam chowder. When she saw him, she set her spoon to the side. "Thank goodness, you're here."

The woman he'd come to find wasn't anywhere around. "Where's Jocelyne?"

Mrs. Baker absently pushed the loose strands of her hair back behind her ears. "Oh dear, you just missed her."

"Missed her?" He grabbed Hazel's arms and made her face him. "Where did she go?"

"Why, she's gone out to the lighthouse to complete the spell, where else?"

"Alone?"

"She insisted, said she wanted the time to think." Hazel wrung her hands together. "I shouldn't have let her go. I knew it." She strode toward the door, grabbing her jacket as she went. "I have to go after her."

"No, I'll go." Andrei followed her across the floor and laid a hand on her arm. "You stay here in case she gets back while I'm out."

The older woman stared through the glass on the back door. "Hurry, then. It's getting dark out there. I don't want my baby hurt or sick because of me. I couldn't live with myself if something awful happened to her."

Andrei pushed past Hazel and out into the wicked wind and rain. He couldn't live with himself if something happened to Jocelyne, either. He jumped into his car and raced out of the gravel parking area and through the deserted streets of Raven's Cliff. Not as if he'd get a ticket for speeding on a night like tonight. No one dared get out in this nasty weather. But what possessed Jocelyne to venture forth wasn't hard to guess.

The crowd had been ugly and the things they'd said hurtful. Jocelyne had to be aching. And for some reason, what made Jocelyne ache, made Andrei ache just as badly. He didn't like the idea of her being out in this storm, especially up by the old lighthouse. A spooky enough place without having part of its structure charred and ragged.

When he slowed to take the turn onto the road leading to Beacon Manor and the lighthouse, a flash of light reflected off the chrome bumper of a car stuck in the ditch ahead. His heart stuttered when he recognized the compact car as the one Jocelyne drove. He pressed the accelerator roaring forward, then hit the brake, bringing his car to a slippery stop behind Jocelyne's. Was she hurt? Was the baby hurt?

Andrei leaped from his car and ran through the rain to the driver's door, praying for the reassuring face of the woman who'd place herself in danger to save others. He couldn't decide whether she was brave or just stupid to get herself into such crazy situations. Soaked and cold, he swiped at the drenched window and looked inside. The car was empty.

Darkness cloaked the landscape, the only light coming from his car's headlights. Where was she? Had she gotten out and walked the rest of the way to the lighthouse or had the Seaside Strangler nabbed her and taken her off as his next sacrifice to the sea?

A sick feeling settled in Andrei's gut. He ran back to his

car, shifted into Reverse, backing to the lighthouse road. When he turned onto the road, he gunned the accelerator and fishtailed until his vehicle straightened.

The driving rain blocked his view of the lighthouse until he was almost on top of it. The old white structure appeared before him, large and looming, its blackened top a grim reminder of an ill-fated night. The night when two people lost their lives trying to light the beacon on the anniversary of the death of Captain Raven's family.

The windshield wipers worked furiously, unable to keep up with the torrential rain, making his view of the structure a blur of motion. He couldn't see light in or around it, but that didn't mean Jocelyne wasn't there. Andrei pushed the car door open and it immediately slammed back in his face. The winds off the sea held him captive in the cocoon of his car. Bracing himself, he shoved against the door, struggling against sixty- and seventy-mile-an-hour salt-laden gusts of wind and rain. He eased out of his car and let the door slam shut as he ran for the lighthouse.

Rain pelted him, blinding him, drenching his jacket and trousers. Leaning his shoulder against the door, he pushed. It budged two inches, then pushed back. Someone was on the other side.

Andrei pounded against the door. "Jocelyne? It's me, Andrei, let me in!" he shouted above the raging storm.

The door gave way with the help of a hefty gust and Jocelyne stood inside, her eyes wide, her hair hanging in limp strands around her pale face. "Andrei?" She fell into his arms, her own wrapping around his waist, her face pressing against his chest. "I thought it might be the Seaside Strangler."

Andrei held her, the cold wind and rain pounding against his back. "It's okay," he said, more to himself than to her, relieved to have found her unharmed.

At last, he managed to move her farther into the lighthouse and closed the door behind him. Filled with the scent of wet stone and the lingering acrid odor of damp, burned wood, the interior room of the lighthouse was fairly dry, except where the rain had soaked the cobbled floor. The door to the long staircase and the one to the outside insulated the couple from the gale-force winds, protecting them from the violence of the storm and the sea breaking against the rocks below the cliff.

When Andrei's vision adjusted to the near darkness, he noticed the flashlight lying on the floor, the beam casting a ray of light toward the staircase. Candles sat in a broad circle around the small room, only one remaining lit.

He pushed Jocelyne to arm's length, smoothing the hair out of her eyes with one hand. "What are you doing here?"

"I promised my mother I'd finish the spell to lift the curse of Raven's Cliff." Jocelyne shrugged, a mirthless laugh rising from her throat. "Seems like the curse lives on by the looks of the weather out there. But I fulfilled my promise by performing the ritual." She stared around at the candles, the now empty bucket and the sheet of paper blown against the wall. "There was a time I swore I'd never delve into witchcraft. But with the way things have been going, I'm beginning to grasp at straws, even Wiccan straws." She glanced up at him, her breath catching on her lips, as if realizing for the first time just how close they were in the small room. "Come on, let's get out of here." When she made a motion as if to move around him, he blocked her way.

Andrei's grip tightened on her arms. "Unfortunately, we're not going anywhere. If it's not a hurricane out there, it's damn near one. We'll wait out the storm until it's safe to drive again."

"That could take hours!" Her eyes rounded and she backed out of his arms, rubbing her hands where he'd gripped her. "I—we can't stay here that long."

"Why not?" He closed the short distance between them. "A minute ago, you were glad to see me. Now you're running again."

Her gaze dropped to his wet shoes. "You know why."

He reached out and lifted her chin, forcing her to look at him. "Because you're afraid I might fall in love with you? Or that you'll fall in love with me?"

Shiny tears welled in her emerald-green eyes. "I'm afraid you'll fall in love with me."

"If that's the case, you might be a little late. I'm well on my way there already."

Her eyes widened and her mouth formed a rounded O. "No! I'm a black widow. You know that. Only a fool would dare fall in love with me."

"Then call me a fool." He grasped her arms again and hauled her against his damp chest. His lips closed over hers in a long soul-defining kiss that sealed his fate and heart.

At first, she remained stiff, her hands flat against his cold and slippery jacket, pushing against him. But not for long.

When her body relaxed, and she melted against him, Andrei wanted to gather her even closer, but their damp cold jackets were in the way.

He broke off the kiss, pressing his lips to her cool forehead.

A shiver shook her body and her face pressed into his neck.

As much as he didn't want to move and break contact with her, Andrei knew they had to get dry and warm or they'd suffer from hypothermia by the time the storm abated. "I'll be right back." After a kiss to the tip of her nose, he jerked the door open and dashed out.

Immediately, the wind struck him, knocking him to his knees. Struggling to his feet, he set off for the car, where he inserted his key into the trunk. Inside was a large, black, plastic trash bag filled with emergency supplies in case of bad weather. Andrei would consider the current storm bad weather, some of the worst he'd seen in a long time. He slung the bag over his shoulder, slammed the trunk and, leaning against the wind, ran back to the lighthouse.

When he burst through the door, Jocelyne was there to slam it behind him.

He pulled out a sleeping bag, a portable lantern and a box of granola bars.

"A veritable treasure trove," Jocelyne said through her chattering teeth.

"The temp's really dropping. You need to get out of the wet stuff and into the bag." When Jocelyne's hands hesitated at the neckline of her coat, Andrei gently brushed her fingers aside and unzipped her jacket, hanging it on the handrail leading up into the lighthouse.

She shivered, rubbing her hands over her arms. "I th-think the temperature has already dropped below forty. But I can't take your bag. You need it as much as I do."

"It's an extra-large bag. It'll fit both of us." He divested himself of his coat, hiding a smile from her.

She was cold and scared and his strongest impulse was to take her into his arms and hold her until all the bad stuff disappeared. And based on their kiss, she wouldn't argue much.

His blood warmed as he untied his boots and slipped them off.

Since Jocelyne wasn't moving, he bent and slipped her damp shoes from her feet. Then he crawled into the sleeping bag and patted the space beside him. "Come on. It's warm in here."

"I'll bet it is." Her teeth chattering, Jocelyne still hesitated.

Andrei got to his knees and reached for her hand. "If not for yourself, think of the baby. You can't afford to get sick on account of your pride."

HIS HAND WAS CALLOUSED, warm and strong, and he drew her down to the sleeping bag.

Too cold and tired to fight him, she climbed in between the layers of down-filled fabric and let Andrei zip it closed around them.

With the warm glow of the lantern chasing away any lingering ghosts, Jocelyne snuggled into the crook of Andrei's arm. High above them the wind wailed through the gaps in the upper levels of the lighthouse, as if sobbing for the lives lost at sea and in the tower.

As she inhaled Andrei's musky cologne and the all-male scent of his skin, just one shirt-layer away from her nose, Jocelyne sighed. "This doesn't change anything. I can't let any man love me. No matter what." She turned her face into his chest and reveled in his warmth, her hand sliding across to the buttons, flicking them open, one at a time.

"It's not your choice."

"Yes it is." She worked her way past all the buttons, laying open his shirt inside the sleeping bag. "I could make you hate me."

"Not possible." His free hand slipped down her arm to her hip.

Her hand slid into the crisp curls scattered across his chest. "I'm carrying another man's child. Doesn't that turn you off in the least?"

The hand on her hip skimmed across the belly, ducking inside the elastic waistline. His fingers splayed across her tightening skin, over the child expanding her belly, month by month. "I think you're sexy and beautiful. The baby inside you is a part of you, a part of your beauty."

She couldn't stop the snowball rolling downhill now. Not when her fingers burned to touch him, to hold him. "You're not making it easy for me to reject you."

"Good." He leaned over, rolling her to her back. "I want it

to be just as hard as you make me." Then he was kissing her, his mouth slanting over hers, his tongue pushing past her teeth to twist and tangle with hers.

Jocelyne gave up the fight, her arms circling his waist, pulling him closer. "I want you so much, I can't think straight," she said into his mouth, losing herself to his kiss, his hands on her body. Most of all, she'd lost herself to the storm raging outside and in her heart.

She pushed against him until he rolled to his side, bringing her with him. Her hands skimmed over his shoulders, shoving the shirt off his back and down his arms.

He helped her out of the black pullover turtleneck and black lace bra. Their jeans were more of a challenge, trapped as they were inside the warmth of the sleeping bag. But after a lot of jostling and wrestling, Jocelyne lay back naked, laughing and kissing Andrei, her internal fire growing more intense with each passing moment. "You don't know what you're getting yourself into with me."

"My eyes are wide-open. I don't believe in curses." He brushed a kiss across her lips and down to the base of her neck. "I believe in you and me." He skimmed his mouth across her skin, searing a path to her left breast, and the puckered nipple rose in offering. He accepted, sucking it into his mouth.

Jocelyne's back arched, every nerve ending screaming for more. "What about tomorrow?"

"I'll take my chances." And he nudged her thighs apart and took her in one long, slow movement, sliding deep inside her. He filled her, stretching her until she cried out.

Andrei froze, his body tense. "Did I hurt you?"

"No," she gasped. "I just didn't know how good it would be. Please…" Her hips rose toward him, inviting him to continue, and she fell into the primal rhythm, meeting him stroke for stroke. When her body teetered on the edge, bursts of sensation sent her toppling over. She spiraled out of control, her fingers digging into Andrei's shoulder.

He tensed in response, pumping into her faster and faster, ever careful not to harm her baby. When he lurched to a stop, he dragged in a deep breath and held it, his member twitching as his seed spilled inside her.

For the moment, Jocelyne dared to let herself live in the moment, forgetting tomorrow and the consequences of her actions. For a moment she dared to believe there was a future for her burgeoning feelings for this man who'd just taken her to heaven and back.

Chapter Fifteen

A cell phone chirped in the darkness, waking Andrei from a light sleep. He tried to move, but one arm was trapped beneath a warm body.

In the dark, stray strands of hair, the scent of herbal shampoo and clam chowder filled his senses, and he remembered. He reached over his head and dragged his jacket from where it hung on the handrail of the lighthouse. The ringing continued until he fished the cell phone from one of his pockets. "Yeah."

"Lagios, this is Captain Swanson, you weather the storm all right?"

Jocelyne stirred, rolling off his arm, and Andrei sat up, the cool air jolting him awake more effectively than a steaming cup of coffee. Not that he wouldn't give his right arm for a cup of java.

"Yeah, we—I did fine. What's up, Captain?"

"Got a match on one of the hairs you brought us yesterday. I need you in ASAP."

"Yes, sir." He flipped the phone shut and a chill raced down his naked back.

"Did he say which one it was?" Jocelyne sat up next to him, pulling the sleeping bag up over her naked breasts.

"You heard?"

"Hard not to when you're this close."

He was suddenly aware of her naked thigh against his and he groaned, rolling over and taking her back into the warmth of the bag. "I'd rather stay with you."

"But you can't." She wrapped a calf around his, sliding her foot up the back of his leg and back down.

Andrei nuzzled the sensitive spot beneath her ear, lavishing kisses across her cheekbone until he took her lips in a long, desperate claim. The storm had passed and their time together was over.

"I have to go to work." He gently nipped at her bottom lip. "But I'm afraid to let you out of my sight."

"Why?"

"I'm afraid you'll go back to thinking we're all wrong for each other."

"We ar—"

He laid a finger across her kiss-swollen lips. "No, we're not wrong for each other. Let me take you out tonight to prove it."

Her golden-red brows dipped inward. "I don't know."

"Promise or I won't tell you where I hid your clothes."

"My clothes are at the bottom of the sleeping bag where I put them."

"Please."

She sighed, then nodded. "Although it's against my better judgment."

He smiled, kissed her with a loud smacking noise and leaped to his feet. "Get up and get dressed, woman. I'm not leaving you here to languish in luxury."

Jocelyne snorted. "You have a strange understanding of luxury."

The dismal interior of the lighthouse couldn't dampen his spirit. He'd just made love to the most beautiful woman he'd ever met and they might have finally found his sister's killer. Justice for Sofia, Angela, Cora and Rebecca—the victims.

He had to hurry. The captain sounded pretty excited about the match and with Jocelyne agreeing to meet him later, he could concentrate on the case without worrying about leaving her. He'd see her later.

Dressed in seconds, Andrei waited for Jocelyne to finish and then ushered her out to his car. "I'll send a wrecker to get your car out of the ditch. But for now, you need to get back to the inn. I'm sure your mother's worried about you." He handed her the cell phone he'd left in the car during last night's storm. "Call her and let her know you're on your way."

She dialed, leaving a message with Leah to tell her mother she'd been holed up with a friend during the storm.

Andrei grinned. *Friend.* That and a whole lot more. Her mother wasn't a fool. She'd figure out the truth soon enough. For now, ignorance meant fewer questions.

When he pulled up outside Cliffside Inn, he shifted into Park.

"You need to go. I'll see you later." Jocelyne was out of the car and through the front door before Andrei could stop her. Just as well, he had a lot to say to her later, after he took care of the case, captured a killer and set the town's worries to rest. Perhaps the spell Jocelyne wove last night in her mother's place had actually worked.

Anticipation surged through him at the thought of capturing the Seaside Strangler. Along with the expectation of closing this case was a deep, gut-wrenching regret that they hadn't caught the killer before he'd taken Andrei's little sister or the other victims. What caused a person to kill innocents?

Andrei hurried up the steps to the police station, brushing past the sergeant on the front desk, who tried to stop him. "Hey you can't go back there."

"Got a meeting with Swanson," Andrei called out over his shoulder, without slowing. The RCPD would know within minutes that he was back on the job. And he didn't care. If what the captain said was true, they as good as had their killer.

Swanson stood in his office, the phone against his ear. When he caught sight of Andrei, he nodded him through the door.

"Yes, Mayor Wells, I've got Mitch bringing the suspect in now." He hung up and stared across his desk at Andrei. "Mitch Chapman is bringing our match in now for questioning. If we can get him to volunteer a hair, we have him."

"Have who?" Andrei held his breath, his mind racing through the four possibilities. His money was on Jackson, the town recluse.

"Ingram Jackson."

A flash of mixed feelings washed over Andrei. The first being that he was right, followed closely by the thought that Jocelyne had been in the same house as a killer. That left him weak-kneed. "You sure it's him?"

"The medical examiner got right on the samples as soon as I sent them over. He's ninety-nine percent sure Ingram's hair matches the one found on Angela Wheeler's bracelet. He's already sent it on to the state crime lab. Now all we have to do is get Ingram to talk and volunteer a hair sample to make it all legal."

"What if he refuses? On what grounds will you hold him?"

"We have one other witness and maybe something will surface in the interrogation. We can't let him slip through the system on a technicality." The captain gave him a grim smile.

Andrei's blood pressure rose at the possibility of the murderer getting off on a technicality. No way in hell would he let the man walk. In the town's current mood, Ingram might not make it to trial. The man had kept them all living in terror for long enough. If he really was the killer, he deserved a little old-fashioned justice. But Andrei's duty was to uphold the law. Sometimes he hated his job. Sometimes justice didn't get served.

When Mitch Chapman walked Ingram Jackson into the

station, it seemed as if the word had gotten out and every police officer on the force, on duty and off, had gathered.

Jackson wore the hooded cape Andrei had seen hanging in the hallway at his house, the hood pulled down low over his eyes, hiding him from view.

Mitch glared at the gauntlet of uniformed and plain-clothes police officers, daring someone to make a move or say something to his prisoner. "This way, Mr. Jackson." He led the prime suspect to the interrogation room.

Andrei sat behind the two-way mirror. "Let me interview him, Captain."

"No way. You're too close to this case. I almost think the entire force is too close to this case. It's hard to think straight after so many have died." He straightened his uniform tie and stepped to the door, turning back to Andrei with his finger pointed. "Stay here. I don't want some defense attorney saying we handled this wrong. If Jackson did it, we can't afford to let him off on a technicality." His narrow-eyed glare bore into Andrei. "Do you understand?"

Andrei nodded, his attention redirected to the man in the other room even before the door closed behind the captain. He wanted his sister's killer bad enough to keep his cool and do it right.

Captain Swanson strode into the other room behind the glass. The man at the bare table twisted his head to look at who entered. "What's going on? Why am I being held?"

Captain Swanson raised a hand. "We have a few questions for you."

"Why couldn't you ask them at my house?"

"Mr. Jackson, where were you the night of Angela Wheeler's disappearance?"

Jackson sat as still as a statue and a long space of silence greeted the captain's question. "I was at my house all night. Alone."

"Can anyone place you at your house?"

"No. My housekeeper leaves at five in the evening and doesn't return until the following morning."

"We've already spoken to your housekeeper. She claims she had to clean up a lot of sand and mud in the hallway the morning after Miss Wheeler's disappearance. Can you explain that?"

Andrei hadn't heard about the housekeeper's testimony. Not that a little sand in the entranceway was an admission of guilt.

"Sometimes I walk at night. I have difficulty sleeping." He leaned forward. "I didn't kill Angela Wheeler or any of those women."

"We have DNA evidence found on the latest victim. Would you be willing to provide us with a hair from your head to compare with what we found?"

His breath held in his throat, Andrei counted the seconds until the suspect answered.

Jackson leaned back, the hood still firmly in place. "Absolutely. I have nothing to hide."

Andrei studied the man from the other side of the mirrored wall. The hood hid scars. What else did it hide?

Ingram Jackson reached beneath his hood and yanked out a hair. "Will this do?"

They had it.

A rush of relief washed over Andrei.

With the legal evidence they needed to arrest the Seaside Strangler, the streets of Raven's Cliff would finally be free of a monster.

The captain removed a surgical glove from his pocket and an evidence bag. He stretched the glove over his right hand and took the hair from Jackson, slipping it into the bag. "I'll be back." He left the room.

Jackson stood and made a circle in the room, coming to a halt in front of the mirrored wall. He stared into it as if he could see through to Andrei on the other side.

All Andrei could see were the electric-blue eyes staring out of the shadowed hood. Something in their depths spoke of tragedy, sadness, loss. A cold ripple spread from the base of Andrei's neck down his back. What if he wasn't the killer? What if they were wrong? Jackson hadn't hesitated to hand over the hair.

Captain Swanson entered the room in which Andrei stood. "Mitch Chapman is running the hair to the clinic. Gordon is in town on standby borrowing the clinic microscopes, just for us," he said, his voice low so as not to carry through to the other room.

Andrei continued to stare into the blue eyes, his own narrowing. "How long?"

"Should only take a few minutes for him to make a positive identification. He's waiting at the clinic in town to get it done and call me right back." Swanson stepped up beside Andrei and stared at the man in the interrogation room. "I couldn't tell anything from his expressions since he had that hood on all the time."

"He sounded certain that he didn't commit the crimes."

"Serial killers can be very convincing."

"Yeah, and deadly." The image of his sister's body washed up on the rocks made Andrei's stomach lurch.

There was a soft tap on the door and the desk sergeant poked his head inside, a grim smile on his face. "The ME called. The hair matches the one found on Angela Wheeler."

Swanson closed his eyes, dragged in a deep breath and let it out before he opened his eyes again. "Book him."

"I'll do it." Andrei dragged his gaze away from the man staring into the mirror. If anyone had the right to arrest the killer, it was him. He'd do it for Sofia. He stepped out of the observation room and into the interrogation room. "Mr. Jackson, I'm Officer Andrei Lagios. You're under arrest for the murder of Angela Wheeler."

"But I didn't do it! On what basis are you arresting me?"

"We have evidence that links you to the Seaside Strangler murders."

"I tell you, I didn't do it. I've never even met Angela Wheeler."

When Andrei snapped the cuffs on Jackson, the man didn't fight back.

"I want to call my lawyer."

"You'll have the opportunity." For the past few months Andrei had envisioned the day they caught the killer. But the relief and closure of jailing the bastard who'd killed his sister wasn't there, and he couldn't understand why. He should be happy to finally have the Seaside Strangler behind bars.

As Jackson passed through the door, his gaze connected with Andrei's. "You've made a big mistake."

"ANDREI!" JOCELYNE hurried down the sweeping staircase of Cliffside Inn two mornings later, jamming her arms into her coat as she went. "I thought you'd moved out yesterday."

"I did." Andrei paused in the front doorway and smiled up at her. "But I missed your mother's cooking." He wore his official Raven's Cliff police uniform, the one saved for special occasions. He stood straight and tall, his hair combed neatly and his face clean-shaven.

"Are you on your way to the arraignment of the Seaside Strangler?" she asked, pushing through the door ahead of him.

"Yes."

They hadn't spoken since he'd dropped her off at the inn two days ago. He'd left a message with Leah to cancel their date for that night. Because of the death threats to Jackson, he'd stayed at the jailhouse late into the night and most of the next day.

Unfortunately, the time away from him had given her entirely too much time to think. With Andrei, thinking wasn't an option. Without him around to kiss her and hold her close, all her fears and worries resurfaced, plaguing her with doubt.

Now that she stood next to him, her doubts disappeared and a warm wash of memories from their stormy night in the lighthouse filled her with an ache that physically hurt in her chest. "I missed you."

He cupped her arm in his hand and squeezed. "We still need to talk. But not until this is over. Can you meet me for dinner?"

A thrill of hope chased away the remaining fear and doubt. "Yes."

A crowd gathered around the police station where the local jail stood. A television station van was parked against the curb and another from Bangor moved into position farther down the street. A female journalist faced a camera in the cool wind, wearing a short skirt and an insubstantial jacket. "We're standing outside the Raven's Cliff jail awaiting our first glimpse of the Seaside Strangler, the man reported to have killed four young women, setting them adrift in the sea in a bizarre ritual."

The door to the police station opened and Captain Swanson stepped out.

"Sir, could you tell us more about the arrest of the Seaside Strangler?"

"We've arrested a suspect in the Angela Wheeler murder case. But I'd like to remind the press that a man is innocent until proven guilty." He moved on, followed by Mitch Chapman and the suspect.

A gasp rose from the crowd. One woman screamed.

"What's going on?" Jocelyne stood on her tiptoes trying to see over the heads of the people surging toward the courthouse and the morning's arraignment.

Andrei's lips thinned into a line. "Ingram Jackson has severe burn scars on his face."

"That's right. He came to Mom for her balm. She said it kept the scar tissue supple."

"He's a monster!" a woman cried out.

"The legal system won't do justice." A stout fisherman shouted a warning.

The newswoman shoved her way into the crowd, moving with the flow of people to the courthouse.

Jocelyne's stomach churned, giving her that old feeling of morning sickness she hadn't experienced since the first trimester of her pregnancy. "I almost feel sorry for the man."

"If he's the strangler, you shouldn't feel sorry for him."

If. Jocelyne's glance darted to the man standing stiff and unbending at her side. His gaze followed the crowd pushing toward the courthouse. "Is there any doubt? I thought the hair was pretty damning evidence."

"It's sufficient evidence for an arrest." Andrei stepped out, following the crowd at a distance. "And thanks to the crime lab working overtime, we know the DNA is a close match."

Jocelyne hurried to catch up. "But you're having doubts?"

"No."

"Yes, you are." She laid a hand on his arm. "Why?"

He stopped, but he didn't look into her eyes. "I don't know. Call it a gut feeling."

"You can't convince a jury on gut feelings. That's where the evidence comes in."

This wasn't right. Andrei knew it, but he couldn't prove it. "I know. Just forget it." He continued on toward the courthouse, without uttering another word.

Jocelyne stood next to Andrei in the back of the courtroom as the judge charged Ingram Jackson with one count of murder. Jackson, with his lawyer by his side, pleaded not guilty. Then the judge denied him bail, stating that if he was in fact the Seaside Strangler, he was a flight risk and too dangerous to the community to let him out on bail.

Shouts rose from the spectators in the courtroom.

"He's guilty!"

"Finally, this town will be rid of evil!"

"Kill the monster!"

"Justice for the lost women of Raven's Cliff!"

The judge banged his gavel and shouted above the noise, "Order! Order!"

A phalanx of police officers crowded around Ingram Jackson, creating a wall of muscles between him and the rabid crowd.

Jocelyne didn't say anything when Andrei left her side to help the others make a path toward the doorway. She stood back against the wall until Jackson and his lawyer left and the contents of the courtroom poured through the door.

Fighting back panic, Jocelyne hugged the wall, her arms wrapped protectively around her belly to keep flying elbows and killer purses from jabbing her baby.

When she finally exited the courthouse, she looked for Andrei. Her shoulders sagged when she realized he'd probably gone on to the police station with the others. He'd mentioned something about having to pull a real shift after being undercover for so long.

Jocelyne would just be in the way if she tried to follow.

Now that the killer had been caught, maybe the town would settle down and life would get on as usual in the small coastal town in Maine. Andrei would go back to being a cop.

And Jocelyne would be alone.

An icy finger scraped her spine. Was it the cool breeze blowing in from the open doorway, or a chilling premonition that all was still not well in Raven's Cliff?

Chapter Sixteen

"I know you've been working case paperwork all day, but if you could hang around the jail this evening until the natives settle, I'd be grateful. Can't have vigilantes taking the law into their hands and disposing of our suspect before his trial." Captain Swanson straightened his tie and ran his fingers over his shiny bald head.

Much as Andrei would love to put the Seaside Strangler away, Andrei's sense of justice fought back. The man deserved a trial. "I'll stay."

"Good. You can leave when I get back. I'll be with the mayor giving a statement to the press." Captain Swanson sighed. "God, I hate cameras."

"Maybe, but you'll give it to them straight," Andrei said automatically. His mind was already in the basement with their prime suspect. He wanted to ask the man a few questions of his own. Something just wasn't sitting right with Andrei about Ingram Jackson. The man didn't act like a nutcase or deeply disturbed serial killer. He acted more like a man being falsely accused and saddened by the way the town treated him.

Acid churned in Andrei's belly. What if they were wrong?

Captain Swanson left, muttering something about the press and twisting words.

Unable to stand in one place for more than a minute, Andrei wound his way through the station to the back staircase that descended into the basement. A block of cells, each with a cot, a toilet and a washbasin, lined the back wall. One officer pulled duty when a prisoner was present. Normally, the cells were empty, except for the occasional drunk in need of a place to sleep it off. Today, they had a special inmate.

Mitch Chapman sat at the old metal desk, polishing his nine-millimeter pistol. "Our prisoner already has a visitor. I put them in the visitors' room." He glanced at his watch. "They have five minutes."

"His lawyer?"

"No, that guy left right after we locked him up. Said something about seeing a senator or something to get the judge to set bail."

"Anybody I know?" Andrei asked.

With a glance down at the sign-in sheet, Mitch answered, "Know an Alex Gibson?"

The skin on the back of Andrei's neck crawled, but he couldn't put his finger on why. "Yeah. He's a fisherman who lives at Cliffside Inn. What's he want with Jackson?"

"I don't know. Gibson said Jackson was family and would want to see him." Mitch shrugged. "Figured it wouldn't hurt as long as he wasn't carrying a concealed weapon. I patted him down and ran the wand over him."

"Good. Do you mind if I check it out?" Andrei moved toward the visitors' room.

"Knock yourself out." Mitch checked his watch again. "In three minutes you can bring Gibson out."

"Will do." Andrei stepped into the whitewashed hallway and peered through the window on the door to the visitors' room. A wall split the room in two, one half for prisoners, the other for visitors, disallowing any physical contact. Bulletproof

Plexiglas stood between Alex Gibson and Ingram Jackson with an intercom system they could communicate through.

Without the hood shadowing his face, Ingram Jackson's scars stood out, a ragged reminder of some terrible tragedy. His brown hair was longer than Gibson's but the same rich-brown color.

They sat with their heads bent close to the dividing wall, Gibson speaking fast, Jackson looking confused.

Andrei switched on the speaker so that he could listen to whatever Gibson was saying.

"Don't you remember?" Gibson asked, his tone urgent and a little angry.

"No. Should I?"

Gibson snorted. "Yes, you should. We were close, inseparable, always sharing our adventures, running wild over the estate."

Ingram frowned, his eyes squeezing shut. "I remember someone I used to play with." His eyes widened and he stared across at Gibson. "Was that you?"

Gibson leaned forward, his hands gripping the edge of the table. "Yes."

Jackson's gaze narrowed. "I always felt as if I could see someone else in my dreams. I had nightmares about a boy just like me." He pinched the bridge of his nose, his forehead creasing.

"So did I. I could feel when he was happy, when he was angry or in pain." Alex's hand rose to his face.

Jackson's hand mirrored the man across from him. "The nightmares had gone away for a long time, then they came back. Recently." His hand dropped and he stared at his visitor. "I could see the strangler, feel his hands on the women's throat, hear the crash of the waves as the body floated out to sea. I could feel it, just as though it was my hands touching them."

Stunned by the strange drama unfolding, Andrei might

have moved. He didn't know for certain if it was his movement or something more subliminal.

Suddenly Gibson shot a glance toward him, his bright blue eyes narrowed to slits.

Jackson's face turned toward Andrei as well, his equally blue eyes wide and curious. Ingram's face was like that of a harlequin, one side scarred and frightening, the other perfectly normal, almost handsome.

Gibson stood, followed by Jackson, both the same height.

The fisherman nodded at the man on the other side of the divider. "We'll talk later." Without waiting for a response, he stalked toward the door and Andrei. Andrei unlocked the door and let him out.

"My time's up, right?" Again, he didn't wait for an answer, just walked through to where Mitch scrambled to gather Gibson's belongings he'd had to surrender from his pockets before he was allowed into the visitors' room. One of the items was a silver ring with the symbol of a pentagram etched in delicate detail. He slid the ring on his finger, coins and keys into his pocket, and left.

For a full minute after the door closed behind Gibson, Andrei stared at where the man had stood. What had been gnawing at him finally blossomed and clicked in Andrei's head. The brown hair and blue eyes should have triggered alarm bells. Combine that with the height, and bingo. "If not for the scars, those two could be—" His head jerked up and he ran for the stairs leading out of the jail.

"What's the matter?" Mitch called out after him.

Andrei didn't slow to respond. Alex Gibson's car headed down Main Street, pulling away into a thickening fog.

Andrei's car was back at the inn. He ran across the square, turning back, trying to see which way Alex Gibson headed. The man turned north before the fog swallowed him.

Andrei sprinted the rest of the way to his car, punching the lock release fifteen yards out. Within moments, he slid behind the wheel, fishtailing out of the parking lot of Cliffside Inn. When his back tires engaged, the car shot onto Main Street in hot pursuit of the fisherman.

If his gut was right, they had the wrong man in jail. If his gut was right, the killer was still on the loose and headed out of town into the rocky hillside in a mist so thick a man could easily lose his pursuer. If Andrei lost him, who would the Seaside Strangler target next? Another innocent like his little sister?

As the miles passed and he climbed farther into the hills, a bad feeling slipped through his chest. He'd lost him. Then a taillight shone ahead of him, traveling at a high rate of speed.

His heart hammering against his ribs, Andrei shoved his foot to the floor picking up speed. Soon the twisting and turning roads forced him to slow. A low bank of fog crept steadily in from the coast, filling the draws and ravines of the hills with their soupy thickness. Soon he was forced to a crawl, afraid that if he met another car coming down, they'd crash head-on. Not that he cared what happened to him, but he couldn't stand the idea of hurting others.

By the time he'd climbed deep into the hills and was a good hour from town, Andrei admitted defeat. He'd lost Alex. For all Andrei knew, Alex could have taken one of the other roads that led beck to Raven's Cliff. The best he could do was get back to town and inform the captain of his suspicions. The only thing that didn't fit was that Alex Gibson had an alibi for every night of every murder. He'd been with his girlfriend all night. People had seen him going into her apartment and coming out the next morning. That's why they hadn't bothered to collect a hair from him.

But if Ingram and Gibson were identical twins, that would explain why the hair matched under the microscope. The idea sounded bizarre enough to be on a television talk show.

*Small coastal Maine town arrests the wrong twin and the real
killer roams free to kill again.*

And the real killer could be on his way back to Raven's
Cliff. Andrei pulled out his cell phone, knowing that this far
out of town the reception would be nil. If he could get a
message to the captain to watch out for Alex Gibson, he'd feel
a lot better. A glance down at his cell phone confirmed that
he didn't have a signal on the screen.

Despite the danger of traversing twisting mountainous
roads in the fog, Andrei pressed his foot to the accelerator,
sticking to his lane but pushing the car to the limits of what
was safe on the fogged-in road.

After thirty minutes of driving the curvy roads, he slowed
to check his signal. Barely registering, but soon he'd have
enough of a signal to place a call to the captain who could
send a unit out to intercept Alex before he made it to Raven's
Cliff.

JOCELYNE'S BACK HURT and the skin across her ever-increasing belly felt tighter than usual. Having searched the kitchen,
she now descended into the basement to find her mother. The
grow lights shone brightly over the plants in the far corner and
a movement caught her eyes. "Mom, I need some of that
balm you've been giving to—"

Instead of her mother, Alex Gibson stepped out of the
shadows, his hair tousled with droplets of water clinging to
the dark-brown strands.

"Is my mother down here?" she asked, wondering what
business Mr. Gibson had in the basement. That she was alone
with the man sent a pinch of fear through her.

"No, I haven't seen her."

Jocelyne moved around the work center where her mother
repotted her plants, keeping the table between her and the man
standing in the lights. "What are you doing down here?"

"Lucy has another of her migraines. I came to get some of the medicinal herbs your mother prescribes for her." He tucked something dark into his pocket before she could properly identify it.

Her mind spinning around other possible reasons Gibson could be alone in the basement, Jocelyne pressed for answers. "Do you know much about the herbs she grows here?"

"I have a great respect for the natural healing arts and the Wicca ways. Your mother has been teaching me a lot of what she knows." His brow cocked upward as if challenging Jocelyne.

Did he know she had refused to learn the Wicca ways? Did he know that she'd rejected her mother's beliefs because of the townsfolk?

Surely her mother wouldn't have told tales about her daughter's quirks. Would she?

Alex's lips turned up in a gentle smile, reminding Jocelyne that he'd been there to defend her mother when the town had turned on her. How could a man so determined to help an outcast be all bad? "When is your baby due, Miss Baker?"

Her hand rose to her belly. "Not for another three months."

"A child is pure and innocent. A blessing. A gift." He rounded the workbench and stood in front of her. "You're lucky, Miss Baker."

With her hand still resting on her belly, Jocelyne stepped backward one step, unsure why, but needing the space. "Yes, I am."

"I can't seem to find what I'm looking for. When you see your mother, would you ask her to please send some of her migraine medicine over to Lucy?" He closed the distance between them and touched her arm. "She's in a great deal of pain. The sooner the better."

"I will. Lucy's lucky to have you to look after her." The man truly cared about his girlfriend's comfort, which brought a warm glow to Jocelyne. Wouldn't it be nice to be cared for like that? But then that would mean a man would have to love her, and she knew where that would lead. Or would it? Had she dreamed up the curse to keep men at arm's length because she was protecting them? Or was she protecting her own heart? Her thoughts strayed to Andrei Lagios. Did she dare fall in love with the cop? Could he fall for a pregnant woman? Could he love her and her baby? Did she want him to have the chance?

The questions spun in circles, making her dizzy. Tears stung her eyelids. Yes. She wanted to love and be loved. If she gave Andrei a chance, would he grow to love her? Did she dare?

"If you'll excuse me, I have to take care of my nets. I'm going out early tomorrow."

Jocelyne jumped. For a moment, she'd lost herself in wishful thinking, forgetting she was still in the basement with Mr. Gibson. "I hope you'll wait for the fog to lift."

"The forecast calls for the fog to lift by morning. If you could make sure Lucy gets her medicine, I'd be grateful."

"I will."

Alex left her standing by the herb garden, deep in thoughts she hadn't dared think since her baby's father died.

Long minutes later, her mother's voice called out from the basement staircase, "Jocelyne? Are you down here?"

Jocelyne pulled herself together and headed her way. "Yes, I'm down here. Alex Gibson came down asking for some of Lucy's migraine remedy."

"Poor girl. She gets them quite often. Yes, I have just what she needs here on the shelf." She rifled through paper packets of ground herbs until she unearthed one marked Migraine. "She'll need it right away. Oh dear, I just sent Leah to the grocery for more flour, and I've got a cake in the oven. Would you be a dear and mind the cake while I run this over to Lucy?"

Jocelyne took the packet from her mother's hands. "Why don't you mind the cake, and I'll take this down to Lucy?"

"Are you sure? The fog's so thick you can hardly see your hand in front of your face. No, I'd better go." She reached for the packet.

Jocelyne held it out of reach. "I know I've been gone for ten years, but I grew up here. I could find my way through these streets blindfolded." She hugged her mother. "I'll be fine. But thanks for worrying about me." She held her mother to her. "I love you, Mom."

Her mother stared into her face, tears glistening on her eyelashes. "I love you, too, baby. Always have."

"And I've always loved you." Jocelyne's mouth twisted into a wry smile. "I may not have said it often enough, but I do. And I plan to change that. I love you, Mom." She kissed her mother's cheek and broke contact, a lump lodged in her throat. If she didn't leave soon, she'd cry. "I'll only be gone a few minutes. If Mr. Lagios shows up, tell him I want to talk to him when I get back."

With a sense of purpose, Jocelyne slung her jacket over her shoulders and stepped out the back door of the inn. For the first time in the six months since Tyler died in the subway accident, Jocelyne dared to hope.

Like her mother said, the fog had consumed the town, making it difficult to see even two feet in front of her. Still, Jocelyne hurried along the street, using the streetlights as her guide. Once she stopped at the corner of a street and stared up at a street sign just to make sure she was headed the right direction.

When she made it to the glass windows of Tidal Treasures, she breathed a sigh, immediately followed by a sense of dread. Last time she'd been down the alley to Lucy's apartment at the rear, she'd been accosted by one of the men who'd jumped the mayor. Maybe she'd have been better off waiting until Andrei came. He could have walked her to Lucy's.

Jocelyne shook her head. She couldn't ask him to play the role of her bodyguard. Now that they had the Seaside Strangler in custody, what did she have to worry about? Squaring her shoulders, she headed down the alley and up the stairs to Lucy's, where she tapped sharply on the wood-paneled door.

"Just a minute!" Lucy's voice called out from the other side of the door. A moment later, she yanked it open, her hair up in a fluffy pink towel, her body wrapped in a teal, silk bathrobe. "Oh, Jocelyne. What are you doing here?" She smiled, her face happy and, as far as Jocelyne could tell, pain-free.

"Alex said you were suffering from another one of your migraines and sent me here with the remedy." Jocelyne held out her hand with the paper package, a frown settling between her eyes. Had Alex been wrong? A cold sensation snaked up the back of Jocelyne's spine.

"Oh, Alex is such a doll." Lucy took the package and placed it in a cabinet over her coffeemaker. "I complained of a slight headache earlier, when we were talking on the phone. He likes to jump right on my migraines. He hates to see me in pain."

Jocelyne let out the breath she hadn't realized she'd been holding. From all she'd seen, Alex Gibson was a nice man. Quiet, for the most part, but he seemed to care for the people around him. He'd proven it over and over by helping her mother and Lucy when they'd needed it. "Do you get the migraines often?"

"No, but some of them are really bad. So bad I can't lift my head off my pillow."

"Have you seen a physician?"

"Oh, yeah. I tracked what food I ate and everything. I still don't know what brings them on. But Alex gives me something to knock me out when I get a really bad one. I sleep like a baby." She held up her hands and smiled. "And the best part is that I don't remember a thing. More importantly I wake up the next morning without a migraine."

That chill slithered across the back of Jocelyne's neck, but she couldn't quite put her finger on what caused it. Lucy's whole attitude about the migraines was too easy. A lot of people with migraines didn't find relief so readily.

"Do you know what Alex gives you? Is it something my mother sends?" She'd have to ask her mother about her super migraine medicine.

"I'm sure that's where he gets it. That's where he gets all his remedies. He thinks your mother is the best. He's always talking about how noble she is for trying to find a cure for the curse and all." Lucy frowned. "A shame the rest of the townspeople didn't see it that way the other day. They were nasty, weren't they?"

"Yes." Jocelyne turned for the door. "I'd better get back."

"Sure you won't stay for tea? I don't get many guests except for Alex." Lucy's gaze looked hopeful.

Lucy's offer touched her. No one had stepped out to befriend her since she'd returned to Raven's Cliff. "I'd love to another time. Right now, I need to get back and help Mom with the dinner crowd."

"I understand. Stop by the shop in the morning and we can talk." Lucy followed her to the door and held it open for her and looked out. "Wow, I didn't realize how foggy it'd gotten out there. Are you sure you'll be all right?"

Jocelyne smiled. "I managed to get here. I can find my way back. Just have to stick to the streets. I'll be fine."

"Call me when you get back to the inn so I know that you made it back all right."

"Okay." Jocelyne smiled at Lucy. "Thanks." Then she climbed down the steps, the light at the top of the landing good for the length of the staircase. Once she reached the bottom, the going got more difficult. The alley was choked in a heavy fog haze.

Jocelyne hurried, feeling her way along the wall of the building, the rough bricks reassuringly solid in the thick bank of fog. She began to wonder if she'd been foolish to come out on a day such as this. Ships crashed into rocks in this kind of weather.

You're not a ship. A tingling sensation spread across her senses and she laughed, trying to shake it off. She felt as if she were being watched, which was ridiculous. Considering she couldn't see her hand in front of her face, how could anyone see her?

Her footsteps echoed on the pavement as she emerged onto the sidewalk. So far so good. Three blocks over and she had it made.

Before she'd even gone one block, she stopped to listen. Was that her footsteps echoing off the brick buildings? Must be an echo because when she stopped, the other sound stopped. She tried to laugh at herself, but the sound came out as a choked whisper. She didn't like to admit it, but damn, she was scared. The chill air crept beneath her jacket and before long, she was shivering uncontrollably, her body shaking so hard her teeth rattled. She tried to tell herself to calm down, but she couldn't, she wanted to be home, safe and sitting in front of the blazing fire.

If she turned at the next corner and cut over a street, she'd come out at the rear of the police station. She could stop in and see if Andrei was there. Maybe he'd walk with her the rest of the way to the inn.

She set off in that direction, about to make the turn when a large dark blob emerged in front of her. A scream rose from her throat, but before it escaped, a gloved hand clamped over her mouth, an acrid scent filling her nostrils. The fog faded to black.

Chapter Seventeen

Finally out of the hills, Andrei slid onto the main road headed south into town. On a straighter road now, he pressed his foot to the floor, eager to get back to town and assure himself Jocelyne was okay.

Before the speedometer climbed up to forty, a large lump of rags appeared on the side of the road. Andrei swerved into the other lane and would have driven on, but something about that pile of rags didn't feel right. What if they weren't rags at all? What if the lump in the road was a body? He'd been fast enough to swerve and miss hitting it. Would the next person?

His pulse hammered in his veins as he skidded to a stop and reversed, backing up until he could see the rags emerge out of the fog. A sickening sensation filled him when he recognized a slim arm stretched out to one side, a long leg and the smooth curve of a hip. He'd found a woman. His world almost crashed in around him like waves pounding against the rocky shoreline. Was he too late? Was it Jocelyne?

Andrei parked and turned on his emergency blinkers, for what they were worth in this fog. Then he was running toward her. When he saw the long, tawny curls, he dropped to his knees, thanking God it wasn't Jocelyne with her straight red hair.

He pressed two fingers to the woman's carotid artery and for a long moment held his breath. He couldn't feel a pulse at first. Just when he was about to give up, a faint beat thrummed against his fingertips.

She was alive, but if she stayed out in this cool, damp air much longer, she'd be dead. He ran his hands over her body, searching for any outward signs of injury. When he found none, he gathered her carefully in his arms and carried her to his car, laying her across the backseat.

When her head tipped back and the overhead interior light shined down in her face, Andrei sucked in a breath. He knew this woman.

Driving slowly, he edged through the fog toward town. As soon as he got a good signal on his cell phone, he dialed Captain Swanson.

"Swanson here." Voices sounded in the background.

"It's Lagios. Are you still with the mayor?"

"Yes. Anything happening at the jail?"

"Something came up, and I had to leave." He paused. "Meet me at the clinic as soon as possible, warn the doctors I'm coming and bring the mayor."

"What's happened?"

"I found Mayor Wells' daughter, Camille." Andrei glanced over his shoulder at the woman, whose face was deathly pale.

"Alive?"

"For the moment." Minutes later, Andrei pulled into the drive-through entrance to the Raven's Cliff clinic. As he jumped out, the clinic's doctors appeared at the door wheeling a gurney.

Dr. Roxanne Peterson leaned into the car and pressed her stethoscope to Camille's chest. "She'd be better off at the hospital."

When she stepped away from the car, Dr. Luke Freeman moved in with the backboard. "Yeah, but you did right to bring her here. We can make sure she's stable until the ambulance arrives."

By the time they had her loaded onto the gurney and were

wheeling her into an examination room, Captain Swanson arrived with Mayor Wells.

"Where is she?" The mayor pushed his way past Andrei and the captain. "Where's my daughter!" He didn't look his normal self. With his hair standing on end as though he'd run his hands through it several times, he wasn't the cool, collected politician. He looked like any other father worried about his daughter.

For a moment, Andrei could set aside his distaste for the man who was suspected of dealing in illegal activities, and took bribes from a man bent on poisoning the people of Raven's Cliff. For now, he was a father relieved to finally find his daughter after she'd been gone for months.

The doctors waved them out of the room, asking them to wait outside while they worked over Camille, inserting an IV and checking her vital signs.

Swanson pulled Andrei aside at the first possible chance. "Spill."

"Alex Gibson." Andrei glanced at his watch. He'd been away from town nearly two hours. The detour to the clinic to deposit Camille had taken longer than he liked. But the captain had to know. "Ingram Jackson had a visitor while you were giving your press conference. A fisherman by the name of Alex Gibson."

"What's a fisherman doing visiting the suspect?"

"He said he was Jackson's relative. Mitch let him in after a full pat down."

Captain Swanson's brows furrowed. "Relative? I didn't know Jackson had any relatives in town. For that matter, I've never seen Gibson and Jackson together."

"I thought it curious as well until I saw the two together." His hands clenched and he stared into the examination room.

The doctors worked with Camille Wells in a desperate attempt to keep her alive until the ambulance could take her to the nearby hospital.

But Andrei didn't see them, his thoughts on the two men he'd witnessed together in the jailhouse. "They both have dark-brown hair, the same color eyes and they're the same height. If not for the scars on Ingram's face, they'd be identical."

"Twins?" Captain Swanson's eyes widened. "You think we have the wrong twin?"

"Yeah. When Gibson left, I tried to follow. I chased him up into the hills along the coast, but lost him."

"Do you think he had anything to do with Camille's disappearance and reappearance?"

Andrei shook his head. "I don't think he had time to collect her and dump her body." He glanced toward the exit. "All I know is that we need to find him and fast. Before he strikes again."

Captain Swanson flipped open his cell phone and punched a single speed dial number. "Send someone out to Cliffside Inn to pick up Alex Gibson. Detain him any way you can. I'll meet the patrolmen there."

Andrei's cell phone vibrated in his pocket. He pulled it out and glanced at the display. The screen indicated an unknown number. Andrei flipped it open. "Yeah."

"Officer Lagios, you have the wrong man." The voice was low, steady and eerily calm.

But the man's quiet compassionate tone froze Andrei's hand and stopped his heart for a second. "Who is this?"

"Some would call me the Seaside Strangler. I like to consider myself a concerned citizen of Raven's Cliff, trying to make a difference."

Captain Swanson mouthed the words, "Is it him?"

Andrei nodded, his pulse speeding. He knew, without the man identifying himself, who it was. "Alex, what have you done?" Why would he call Andrei unless he had something or someone Andrei wanted?

"The sea demands sacrifices."

As soon as Gibson said the words, Andrei understood. He had Jocelyne. If the floor could have opened up and swallowed him, he wouldn't have felt worse. He took a deep breath and in as composed a voice as possible, he insisted, "No, Alex, the sea doesn't demand sacrifices."

"But it does. It started with Captain Raven's family."

"Alex, where are you? Let's talk," Andrei pleaded.

He went on as if Andrei hadn't spoken. "The sea demands innocent lives like those of the Raven children. Their purity appeases the sea's anger. My brother knows. He can feel it."

"Are you talking about Ingram Jackson?"

"Of course. Although it amused me that you put *him* in jail. He had nothing to do with the sacrifices. *I'm* the one responsible for saving Raven's Cliff."

A lead weight settled in Andrei's gut. How did you reason with a man who was completely off his rocker? "What are you doing now, Alex?" Andrei asked, afraid of the answer, but needing to know.

"I'm preparing another gift for the sea. The curse of Raven's Cliff will be lifted when it's all done. Unlike my other sacrifices, this one is not innocent, but she has purity growing within. I must go now. The sea calls."

The call clicked off and Andrei stared down at his cell phone for a long moment.

"What did he say?" Captain Swanson demanded.

"He's going to kill again."

"Who?"

"Jocelyne Baker." He punched in the number for Cliffside Inn.

Hazel Baker answered.

"Mrs. Baker, this is Andrei Lagios. Could I speak to Jocelyne?"

"Oh, Andrei." Her voice trembled. "I sent her out over an hour ago with a remedy for Lucy's migraine. She hasn't returned and Lucy called more than forty-five minutes ago to say she'd left. I'm so afraid something's happened to her."

Andrei felt dead, alone, unable to move. Finally, he forced words through his constricted vocal cords. "Don't worry, Mrs. Baker, we'll find her."

"Oh, thank you. Thank you."

He clicked the phone off to the sound of her sobs.

"He has her, doesn't he?" the captain asked, his brows dipping low.

"Yes."

"Where is he? Did he say where he was going?"

"No." Deep, despairing fear shook Andrei. He had no idea where to look. Then anger surged through him, pumping life and purpose through his system. "He said Jackson knew how it felt. What do you think he meant by that? Do you think Jackson knows where he went?"

"I don't know, but it's worth finding out. Come on." Captain Swanson strode for the exit. "We'll go in my car."

Andrei climbed in beside the captain, his hand gripping the armrest so tightly his fingers turned white. "We have to stop him."

"We will."

Andrei wondered if they would find him in time to save Jocelyne.

JOCELYNE AWOKE IN THE BACKSEAT of a car, her hands tied behind her back, and she was wearing a white wedding dress. The dress alone almost made her heart stop. She fought to get her elbow under her and pushed herself to a sitting position.

Her captor's profile turned her blood to ice. "Alex Gibson."

The glacial-blue gaze connected with hers in the rearview mirror. "Jocelyne. A shame you woke so soon. I didn't want to have to drug you again."

How stupid she'd been to walk alone in the fog. How

stupid to think it could never happen to her when he'd already taken the lives of four other women. She'd placed her unborn child in jeopardy. "So it's been you all this time. Why?"

"I would think you, of all people, would understand. Your mother and I have been trying to break the curse of Raven's Cliff since the night the lighthouse burned."

"I don't understand. The medical examiner was certain the hair found on Angela was the same as the one they got from Mr. Jackson. How could they be so wrong?"

"These people don't know Jackson like I do. They don't know what kind of *family* he came from." Alex's voice grew taut and angry. "He might as well have been a killer, just like his parents. They played favorites with their twin boys and when one of them tried to drown the other in the bath water, they threw him away. Kicked him out of his own home. Gave him up for adoption. How do you suppose a boy feels when he grows up knowing his parents didn't want him? They favored his twin brother so much they'd acted as if the other never existed." The entire time he talked, Alex's foot pressed harder to the accelerator until the car flew along the road, the fog cloaking the curves.

Jocelyne gasped when the road disappeared.

Alex twisted the steering wheel hard to the right, slamming on his brakes. With too much momentum, the back end swung around, sending the vehicle into a three-sixty spin.

Without a seat belt and with her hands tied behind her back, Jocelyne slid off the seat, landing with a jolt on the floorboard. Unable to tell what was happening, she stayed low, in fear for her life and that of her child.

The car crashed in a bone-jarring stop. Metal crunched and her head slammed into the seat in front of her, but cushions protected her from harm. When the world grew still, Jocelyne noticed that the door at her feet had flown open. Jammed between the seats, she struggled to sit up, peering between the front bucket seats.

Alex's body slumped over the steering wheel, and he let out a moan.

In a split second, she was off the floor and diving for the open door and her only chance to escape a madman.

When her feet touched the ground, she stumbled and fell. Before she hit the dirt, she twisted, letting her shoulder take the brunt of the impact. Pain shot through her arm and she groaned.

The driver's door opened, spurring her to action. She tucked her knees under herself and launched herself forward. Staggering to a run, she found the road and raced along the uneven gravel. Where it led she didn't know until a tall white turret loomed out of the mist, its curved walls towering above her into the fog. A scream ripped from her throat as she realized where she was. The Seaside Strangler had brought her to the lighthouse where the curse had begun.

INGRAM JACKSON GLARED at Andrei. "Why should I help you? You accused me of murders I didn't commit, submitted me to public ridicule and threw me in jail." Jackson stood with his chin up, the horrible scars in full view of the men gathered around him.

Andrei suppressed his impatience. The man had a right to be angry, but he was possibly the only one who could lead them to the killer. "If you don't help us, another woman could die. A pregnant woman." He stared across at the other man, refusing to flinch at his ugly deformity. "Please."

For a long moment, Jackson stared at Andrei. "You love her, don't you?"

Did he? Andrei had only known Jocelyne for a few days, how could he have fallen for her so soon? He pictured her standing on the edge of the cliff, alone, independent and feisty. And the night she'd made love to him, she'd pushed him away, unwilling to sacrifice him for her own desires and needs. Then there was her fierce determination to protect her mother, even though her mother's chosen beliefs had caused her to suffer as a child.

"Yes." Andrei nodded. "I love her, and I'd like the chance to tell her."

"I loved a woman once." Jackson hunched his shoulders. "But I made some bad choices. So many times I've wished I could undo my mistakes and do it all over again." He held Andrei's gaze a moment longer, looking through him rather than at him. Then he straightened. "I'll help you. What is it you want me to do?"

"He's your twin, isn't he?" Andrei asked. "Alex Gibson is your twin."

Ingram nodded. "I'd forgotten. We were very young when he disappeared out of my life. My parents never mentioned him and his memory faded." He shook his head. "How do you lose a twin? I grew up in what I thought was a fairly normal family."

Andrei gripped Ingram's arm, cutting through his reminiscing. "You said you could feel when he was angry or mad or…" he inhaled and let it out "…strangling his victim."

Jackson's eyes widened. "I could. I felt every one of them, watched them as they fought to live, and ultimately died." He ran a hand over his face. "I thought they were just nightmares brought on by the news of the women going missing." Ingram's breath came in shallow puffs. "I could even hear the crash of waves on the shore."

"Mr. Jackson…Ingram…can you hear him now?" Andrei held his breath.

"I don't know. Usually, I was in bed or by myself." Jackson closed his eyes.

"Can you—" Captain Swanson started to ask him a question, but Andrei cut him off with a sharp slicing motion.

The station went stone silent while Ingram Jackson stood as still as a statue, the undamaged side of his face pale and troubled, his brow dipping into a frown. "Anger. At me…at our parents…" His entire body jerked and he swayed.

Andrei put out a hand to steady the man. "What do you see?"

"A winding road, a crash. I—he hit his head on something and blacked out for a moment."

"Where are you?" Andrei asked. "Can you see where you are?"

"Fog. Thick, heavy fog." Ingram sucked in a breath. "She's getting away…must catch her."

"Who's getting away? Is it Jocelyne? Is she running?" A surge of hope filled Andrei's chest. Would her independence and desire to live be enough to save her from a man who'd already taken four lives?

"Must…catch…" Jackson's arm reached out. "Foggy, following a road. A road I know." A smile curved on his lips. "She can't get away. She's trapped."

Andrei's blood froze in his veins. The Seaside Strangler had Jocelyne trapped. He could kill her and no one could do anything to stop him. "Where?"

Jackson stood for a moment without answering, his eyes closed tightly. Then they opened and he stared up at Andrei. "The lighthouse."

That's all Andrei needed. He and Captain Swanson were out the door and into the patrol car within seconds. A minute later, they sped out of town along the highway that led to Beacon Manor and the lighthouse. Andrei drove, stretching the limits most sane people would impose on slick, fog-soaked roads. Many times, he slipped rather than maneuvered around sharp turns in the road.

"You're going to give me a heart attack," Captain Swanson muttered through clenched teeth. "But don't slow down. We have to get there."

Andrei had no intention of slowing until he reached the

lighthouse. He recognized a particularly sharp curve close to where he'd turned off onto the private road to the lighthouse. Wheels slipping slightly, he negotiated the road. His fog lights glinted off the metal bumper of a car smashed against a large boulder.

His foot slammed on the brakes and he fishtailed, slowing even more. "Do you think…?" Visions of Jocelyne lying unconscious in the wreckage tortured Andrei's mind and he prepared to jump from the car to investigate.

"No." Captain Swanson laid a hand on his arm. "Ingram said she was running and that his brother was at the lighthouse." The captain waved him forward. "Go!"

The boss was right. Jocelyne had escaped. Whether or not she was still free of the monster, was unknown. They had to get to her. Andrei pounded the accelerator and the car shot onto the gravel road.

JOCELYNE REACHED THE LIGHTHOUSE first, her lungs wheezing and pain ripping through her side. She hadn't jogged in the month since her belly had started to swell.

She pushed through the door into the lighthouse and turned to slam it behind her. Her relief turned to consternation and fear when she remembered that the lock had long been broken. She had no way of keeping the Seaside Strangler from entering.

A quick glance around the confined space yielded nothing but the sleeping bag and candles she and Andrei had left behind. A silent testimony to a night spent in a magical location…a place about to become her worst nightmare.

The doorknob turned, jerking her out of her memories and into her present dilemma. Jocelyne dove for the door just as it pushed open. She hit it with her shoulder, throwing all her weight into it. The sudden impact sent the door slamming closed and for a moment, she'd pushed back her pursuer.

Then, bracing her body against the wooden panels, she pressed her feet against the stone floor, hoping she could hold him off until help arrived.

Surely by now someone would have figured out that Jocelyne Baker wasn't at home. Lucy would have called and asked if she'd made it. Her mother would freak out when time passed and her daughter hadn't come home. She'd call the station and Andrei would be there.

The door lurched against her back. Jocelyne grit her teeth and fought back, the strain making the backs of her thighs and her calves scream.

"Jocelyne, let me in." Alex's muffled voice carried through the thick wood, a pleading, eerie sound. "I have to appease the sea."

Shifting her leverage, Jocelyne pressed her palms against the door. "Like I'm going to let you kill me and my baby? It's murder, Alex," she shouted.

"It's the only way to break the curse. Let me in."

When Alex decided to break through, no matter how hard Jocelyne tried, she wouldn't be able to hold him off. He weighed a lot more than she did and was strong from his life as a fisherman.

A laugh escaped her throat. Alex Gibson had fooled an entire town with his mild-mannered fisherman act. All the time he'd been picking off young women, one by one. Murdering them and burying them at sea. And the scariest thing about it was that he probably believed he was doing the town a favor.

Please, Andrei, get here soon.

Her silent plea was followed by a cold reminder that she'd pushed Andrei away. Why should he care about her after that? Despair welled up in her, weakening her resolve.

At that precise moment, Alex Gibson hit the door with enough force to send Jocelyne flying across the room and onto her knees, screaming as loud as she could, for whatever good it would do. No one would hear her.

It was too late. Jocelyne Baker would be the next sacrifice the Seaside Strangler would offer up to the sea. Her baby would never know how much her mother loved her.

Chapter Eighteen

Andrei eased the car to a halt and shifted into Park.

"I'll have everyone walk from here. If he has her, we'll need the element of surprise on our side. I'll send the others out to surround the sides of the lighthouse. You and I will take point. We'll be the ones to go in. No one is to shoot unless ordered to." He handed Andrei a two-way radio. "Go, and let us know the situation. And, please, I don't need a dead hero."

Before the captain finished, Andrei grabbed the radio and raced up the road.

The lighthouse had just materialized from the fog when a blood-curdling scream rent the air. From the muffled echo, he'd bet it came from inside the structure. Andrei's hackles rose to full alert at the same time a wave of hesitant relief washed over him. Jocelyne was alive enough to scream, but was it a scream of terror? Was she at that moment being attacked?

Without waiting for the others, Andrei ran for the door, pulling his gun from the holster beneath his arm. He paused outside and listened, but couldn't hear anything above the splash of waves against the rocky coastline, just over the edge of the cliffs. Standing to the side of the door, he shoved it open with his foot, then poked his nine-millimeter pistol into the gap, following it closely. The room was empty, but footsteps clattered on the steps leading up into the tower.

"Alex, give it up. By now, they know it's you. The police will be here soon." Jocelyne's shout sounded from halfway up the stairs.

"I don't have a choice," Gibson shouted. "In order to save the town, an innocent has to be sacrificed. It's the only way."

Andrei took the stairs two at a time, easing up the steps as fast as he could, making as little noise as possible.

The staircase spiraled upward, shooting forty feet into the sky. Another scream split the air. "Let me go!"

Andrei caught up with them just as Alex dove for Jocelyne, snagging her calf on the steps above. He'd shoot the man if he weren't afraid the bullet would ricochet off the walls and hit Jocelyne. Silently, he tucked his weapon into its holster and, before Alex saw him, he threw himself at the man, knocking loose his grip.

Jocelyne scrambled farther up the steps and stopped. "Watch out!"

Both men bumped down the steps on their bellies until they came to a stop. Andrei scrambled to his feet, his hand going to the holster beneath his arm. His pistol had fallen out in their tumble down the steps.

Alex rolled to his feet and pulled a wickedly sharp filet knife from a case on his belt, brandishing it in Andrei's face. "Don't try to stop me, Lagios. The only way to save this town is to feed the sea's appetite."

"You're not taking Jocelyne or anyone else," Alex said in a cool calm voice, while his blood hammered through his veins. "It's over."

"Until the beacon shines again, the curse will live on." Alex lunged for him.

Andrei caught his wrist and twisted, slamming the man against the wall. "Get out, Jocelyne. Now!"

Jocelyne scrambled to her feet and ducked behind Andrei and Alex on the narrow staircase.

"No! You can't let her go," Alex yelled, his desperation fueling him to fight back. He ducked under Andrei's arm and jerked his hand free. The knife fell, clattering down the steps toward Jocelyne, and Alex ran up into the tower.

As soon as she'd moved out of range of the struggling men, Jocelyne had turned and waited.

Andrei paused long enough to see that she hadn't left and he shouted, "Get out! Get out of the lighthouse."

"No. I can't leave you," she called out, bending to retrieve the knife.

With no time to argue, he followed Alex, yelling over his shoulder, "Do it for the baby. You have to protect your child."

When Andrei emerged at the top of the stairs into the burned out hull where the beacon had once stood, he was broadsided.

Like an out-of-control freight train, Alex rammed his shoulder into Andrei's side, knocking him across the small room, slamming him into what was left of the wall.

Andrei struggled to get his feet under him and to catch his breath. The wind had been thoroughly knocked out of him and stabbing pain shot through his side.

Two feet away from him, Alex rose from his knees. "Let me take her. We have to give the sea a sacrifice."

"No. You're done here, Alex." Andrei stalked toward him, pulling handcuffs from his back pocket.

As Andrei advanced, Alex staggered to his feet backing away, solitary tears etching a path from each of his eyes down his cheeks. "You don't understand. Raven's Cliff needs me to do this. It's my home, I love it, and I won't let the curse destroy everything."

When the backs of his legs bumped against the low wall on the seaward side of the lighthouse, Alex glanced over his shoulder. "The sea demands a sacrifice. I was chosen to perform the ceremony." His words came out in a low thoughtful tone as if he'd just learned something wonderful. He turned to stare at Andrei, a smile curving his lips. "It's destiny. I was chosen for this. I will fulfill my duty and my destiny and in so doing, will avenge the wrath of the sea and break the curse."

Andrei reached out to snap the cuffs on Alex, but his hand grasped at air.

In a swift movement, Alex leaned so far backward, he tipped over the edge of the low wall and disappeared into the mist.

THE ONLY REASON JOCELYNE did as Andrei told her was that Captain Swanson raced up the stairwell. With the police force behind Andrei, Jocelyne dragged herself down the steps and outside. Up in the top of the tower, shouts rang out and suddenly all went quiet. The fog had thinned, but she couldn't see what was happening and wished she'd followed the captain.

That's when she saw it. A man's body tumbled out the window facing the sea and cartwheeled through the air.

Jocelyne screamed and fell to her knees as the body crashed into the rocks and waves, sinking beneath the surface.

She bent double and pressed her face to the cool moist grass, a sob welling in her chest to emerge as a long low moan.

The curse. Her curse. Even without clear identification, she knew in her heart, the body that had fallen had been Andrei's. She rolled to her side, the cold damp ground soaking through her clothing, and she shook from head to toe. She knew she should get up and find a warm place, but why? Another man had died because of her. Tears streamed from her eyes and she sobbed, too tired to get up, too tired to live. She closed her eyes and let the waves of grief drown her in their depths.

Strong arms lifted her up from the ground and held her against a solid wall of muscles. A knife slid between her wrists, slicing through her bonds.

Blood rushed into her hands and Jocelyne shook her arms. Angry that she could feel and breathe and live while Andrei lay at the bottom of the ocean, she kept her eyes closed tight, avoiding the truth, avoiding the pain of her loss. Then warm lips pressed to her eyelids. "Please, Jocelyne, open your eyes. Tell me you're okay."

Jocelyne cried out, her arms wrapping around Andrei's neck in a hold so tight, surely she would hurt him. But she couldn't let him go. "Oh, Andrei. I thought you were dead."

"You thought it was me?" A chuckle rumbled in his chest. "You don't have much faith in me, do you?"

She looked up at him through watery eyes and thought she'd never seen a more beautiful man. "But the curse. You're not dead."

"I told you there was nothing to it. It would take more than a curse for me to leave you."

Jocelyne's mouth twisted. "You're sure full of yourself, aren't you?" Her words didn't turn out as sharp and sarcastic as she'd intended, nor could she hide her smile. She pressed her face to his chest and inhaled the salty, musky scent that reminded her of the sea and Raven's Cliff, the town she was learning to love.

"Want me to let you go?" he asked with his lips pressed against her temple.

"No. Not now. Not ever." She cupped his cheek with one hand and angled his face down to hers where she pressed her lips to his in a tentative kiss.

Andrei had other ideas. He eased her to her feet and deepened the kiss, his mouth slanting over hers, his tongue pushing past her lips to stroke her tongue in a deep and mind-numbing caress.

When Jocelyne came up for air, she turned toward the sea, the fog having lifted enough she could see out across the tumultuous waves. "Is it really over?" she asked, her voice a faint sound against the churning tide slapping against the rocky cliffs.

"Yes. It's over." Andrei hugged her to him and they turned toward the other officers gathered around the lighthouse.

Ingram Jackson stared out to the sea, his brow drawn low over his good eye.

His faraway gaze sent a cold tingling sensation over Jocelyne's skin, as though the feet of the dead treaded on her. She paused and gazed out in the direction Ingram looked and she could swear she saw a man suspended above the waves.

But when she blinked, he'd disappeared. Jocelyne's entire body shook, the cold saturating her, making her teeth rattle.

"What is it?" Andrei removed his jacket and wrapped it around her.

"Nothing. Just the cold."

He pressed a kiss to her forehead as he zipped her into his jacket. "Stick with me. I have ways of warming you." His hands slipped around her to cup her belly. "Both of you."

"I never thought of Raven's Cliff as my home." Jocelyne leaned against him, basking in the heat of his body, and the gentle, caring tone of his voice and all the horrors of the past few days faded with the mist. "Until I found you." Then she turned in his arms and kissed him.

* * * * *

THE CURSE OF RAVEN'S CLIFF *still lurks.*
Don't miss Mallory Kane's
SOLVING THE MYSTERIOUS STRANGER
next month, only in Harlequin Intrigue.

The Colton family is back!
Enjoy a sneak preview of
COLTON'S SECRET SERVICE by Marie Ferrarella,
part of THE COLTONS: FAMILY FIRST *miniseries.*

Available from Silhouette Romantic Suspense
in September 2008.

He cautioned himself to be leery. He was human and he'd been conned before. But never by anyone nearly so attractive. Never by anyone he'd felt so attracted to.

In her defense, Nick supposed that Georgie could actually be telling him the truth. That she was a victim in all this. He had his people back in California checking her out, to make sure she was who she said she was and had, as she claimed, not even been near a computer but on the road these last few months that the threats had been made.

In the meantime, he was doing his own checking out. Up close and exceedingly personal. So personal he could feel his blood stirring.

It had been a long time since he'd thought of himself as anything other than a law enforcement agent of one type or other. But Georgeann Grady made him remember that beneath the oaths he had taken and his devotion to duty, there beat the heart of a man.

A man who'd been far too long without the touch of a woman.

He watched as the light from the fireplace caressed the outline of Georgie's small, trim, jean-clad body as she moved about the rustic living room that could have easily come off the set of a Hollywood Western. Except that it was genuine.

As genuine as she claimed to be?

Something inside of him hoped so.

He wasn't supposed to be taking sides. His only interest in being here was to guarantee Senator Joe Colton's safety as the latter continued to make his bid for the presidency. Everything else was supposed to be secondary, but, Nick had to silently admit, that was just a wee bit hard to remember right now.

Earlier, before she'd put her precocious handful of a daughter to bed, Georgie had fed his appetite by whipping up some kind of a delicious concoction out of the vegetables she'd pulled from her garden. Vegetables that, by all rights, should have been withered and dried. She'd mentioned that a friend came by on occasion to weed and tend it. Still, it surprised him that somehow she'd managed to make something mouthwatering out of it.

Almost as mouthwatering as she looked to him right at this moment.

Again, he was reminded of the appetite that hadn't been fed, hadn't been satisfied.

And wasn't going to be, Nick sternly told himself. At least not now. Maybe later, when things took on a more definite shape and all the questions in his head were answered to his satisfaction, there would be time to explore this feeling. This woman. But not now.

Damn it.

"Sorry about the lack of light," Georgie said, breaking into his train of thought as she turned around to face him. If she noticed the way he was looking at her, she gave no indication. "But I don't see a point in paying for electricity if I'm not going to be here. Besides, Emmie really enjoys camping out. She likes roughing it."

"And you?" Nick asked, moving closer to her, so close that a whisper would have trouble fitting in. "What do you like?"

The very breath stopped in Georgie's throat as she looked up at him.

"I think you've got a fair shot of guessing that one," she told him softly.

* * * * *

Be sure to look for COLTON'S SECRET SERVICE and the other following titles from
THE COLTONS: FAMILY FIRST *miniseries:*
RANCHER'S REDEMPTION by Beth Cornelison
THE SHERIFF'S AMNESIAC BRIDE by Linda Conrad
SOLDIER'S SECRET CHILD by Caridad Piñeiro
BABY'S WATCH by Justine Davis
A HERO OF HER OWN by Carla Cassidy

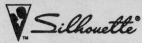

Romantic
SUSPENSE

**Sparked by Danger,
Fueled by Passion.**

The Coltons Are Back!

Marie Ferrarella
Colton's Secret Service

The Coltons: Family First

On a mission to protect a senator, Secret Service agent
Nick Sheffield tracks down a threatening message only
to discover Georgie Gradie Colton, a rodeo-riding single
mom, who insists on her innocence. Nick is instantly
taken with the feisty redhead, but vows not to let his
feelings interfere with his mission. Now he must figure
out if this woman is conning him or if he can trust her
and the passion they share....

Available September wherever books are sold.

**Look for upcoming Colton titles
from Silhouette Romantic Suspense:**

RANCHER'S REDEMPTION by Beth Cornelison, Available October
THE SHERIFF'S AMNESIAC BRIDE by Linda Conrad, Available November
SOLDIER'S SECRET CHILD by Caridad Piñeiro, Available December
BABY'S WATCH by Justine Davis, Available January 2009
A HERO OF HER OWN by Carla Cassidy, Available February 2009

Visit Silhouette Books at www.eHarlequin.com   SRS27598